555

VOLUME 2:
THIS HEAD, THESE LIMBS

CB555-05: 555 Vol. 2: This Head, These Limbs
ISBN: 978-0-9962768-7-0

Carrion Blue 555
Chicopee MA / Lambertville NJ
carrionblue555@gmail.com

"This is Heaven alright, but there's a man outside with a gun."
—Cardiacs, "What Paradise is Like"

TABLE OF CONTENTS

OH CHRIST, NOT THIS SHIT AGAIN
An Introduction by Joseph Bouthiette Jr.
v

A CUT ABOVE THE WRIST
Stephanie M. Wytovich
7

THE DEATH OF ACCOUNTABILITY
Michael Allen Rose
37

GODS OF THE RED RUIN
Tiffany Morris
67

55 WAYS I'D PREFER NOT TO DIE
Michael A. Arnzen
97

ROTTEN BED NUTS
Brian Warfield
127

COPYRIGHT PENDING
John Edward Lawson
157

HEMATOPOIESIS
Amelia Gulbranson
163

APOPTOSIS
Jonathan Moon
193

MISOGYNISTIC TOASTER
Andy de Fonseca
223

DREAMS OF FUTURES PAST
DJ Tyrer
255

THE TASTE OF SALT ON YOUR LIPS
Betty Rocksteady
287

OH CHRIST, NOT THIS SHIT AGAIN
An Introduction by the Series Editor

I'm a big fan of subtitles. When *555 Vol. 1* was being prepared for release, I needed to dub it something worthy of those authors who trusted their work in my hands, who trusted my and Josh's vision for our own press. Amongst the authors in *Vol. 1* are some of my closest friends, and all of them are literary idols. To pretentiously quote myself from the introduction to that volume, there truly were none so worthy.

Vol. 2, naturally, needed its own unique subtitle. *This Head, These Limbs* is perfect—in my totally unbiased opinion—for two reasons: if *Vol. 1* is the central body that established the series, then the stories of *Vol. 2* are the limbs that strike out and bring the series in new directions; also, this volume has a strong lean towards horror fiction, so the visual of heads and limbs scattered about is entirely appropriate.

As always, a huge thank you to all authors and artists who have worked with our press—past, present, and future. Thank you to Matthew Revert whose cover art is always just so damn good. And, of course, the biggest thank you of all to our readers, without whom we'd probably still keep doing this, but it wouldn't be nearly as fun.

This volume is humbly dedicated to the memory of Jimmy Roger Joseph LeBlond.

Joseph Bouthiette Jr.
Summer 2016

A CUT ABOVE THE WRIST

Stephanie M. Wytovich

THE HANDS OF A SEVERED POET

I often think about what it would be like to cut off my hands, to have two stumps that plop and bang rather than fingers that glide over keys, make words and tell stories. I wonder if people would listen to me if I went silent, if they would make poetry with my mute remains.

INSIDE OF ME, SHE BLEEDS

There's a monster in my veins. Her name is my own and she bubbles and bleeds, tries to convince me to let her out, to let her play. Sometimes I make an incision. Just enough to give her a taste. But still she cries, still she screams, screams pleas of amputation, cries operas of pain.

BRUSHING WITH BLOOD

The walls in my room were white, but everything in my mind was red, red like the cherries I ate, red like the pomegranate juice that dripped down my chin. I liked red, liked the way it stained my teeth, the way it complimented my gums when I brushed my teeth with the morning's blood.

OEDIPAL SOLUTIONS

I wasn't happy. The world was ugly and I didn't like what I saw, what I was forced to look at every day. Outside it was bright. It hurt to be alive, hurt to watch. But I felt better when I took out my eyes, because then the world went dark. Then, I could see.

POSTMARK TO PAIN

My body has 555 cuts on its skin, each made with love, each made with careful consideration, for I, myself, am a mailbox of suffering. Learn my address. Postmark your hate mail, send it straight to my heart. This is who I am. I'm made for it. 555 slots for sorrow. I can take it.

DATING MY DEATH WEAPON

Knives are what I know, what I trust. They don't fail me. They don't walk away. In fact, their slim, metal bodies are the best lovers I've known. Dependable. Efficient. Consistent. Their foreplay is torture. Their penetration is climax. When I fuck them, I bleed. When we make love, they write notes on my back.

MAKE ME BLEED, MAKE ME HISS

I wanted to pierce my ears, so I took a needle and shoved it through my lobes. They barely bled, except for a drop or two, so I pierced my nose. When that didn't bleed, I took scissors and cut out a section of my tongue. I swallowed the cube of flesh muscle. Hissed breaths.

HUMAN PINCUSHION

The spikes hugged me in my body drawer, in my metal casket, and I was the Iron Maiden, the girl who slept with the thorns and dressed herself in holes. My skin, polka-dotted and infected, beat shades of red and pink. I dressed my wounds with the tears I laughed. I cried my blood away.

ARSONIST LULLABY

Father Fire sings me my lullaby, his voice burning the world as he lulls me to dream with ashes, tucks me in with flames. When I drift off to sleep, there's a match in my hand, when I wake up in the morning, there's destruction on my breath. I am his death phoenix, his redemption.

DARK ROAST

She cried hard into her coffee when she wanted to mix the cream and sugar, and silently wept into her mug when she took her caffeine black. The trick to a strong cup was the amount of suffering she put into it. If her heart wasn't black enough, the dark roast never came out right.

ELECTROCUTION JUNKIE

The hurricane screamed itself raw with its booming voice and electric words, and the girl took each strike, each hit, as her ragdoll body was flung side to side, beaten and bloody near the front door of her mind. She'd come around. Always did. Most women were made for madness. She was made for storms.

COMMIT THEM TO MEMORY

There's a code to this trade, a set of rules that I follow, rules that keep me on schedule, that prevent me from making mistakes. I never take trophies, have no need for reminders. I commit each detail—every name, every taste, every article of clothing—to memory. I know I'll never forget my girls.

HE'S BETWEEN MY LEGS

I cut his name into my thighs with a piece of broken glass from the bottle I knocked off the desk when he walked away. He was the only man I saw when I spread my legs, so I marked him in flesh, in memory for how he still fucks me even though he's gone.

MY VAGINA IS A ZOMBIE

I don't bleed like a normal woman, because I'm not a normal woman. Every 28 days I hemorrhage until I die, a lifetime of deaths served by the slit between my legs. I have the axe wound that never heals, the river that always runs red. My vagina is a zombie, a reanimated gore machine.

MY MEN DON'T BRING ROSES

If I had to choose between lovers, I would choose the one who scares me, the one who makes my heart beat fast out of fear. I need a partner who's going to bring an axe to the bedroom every once in a while. I like a man who knows how to make me scream.

BLOOD MAPS

I puked razor blades and knives, threw up needles and a pair of shearers, and still my body takes the abuse, still it begs for more, more cuts and incisions, more holes and puncture wounds. When will the blood maps that I've drawn in scars be enough? When will those pictures lead me to recovery?

RED IS MY FAVORITE COLOR

There's something about the color red that gives me peace, that lets me open my lungs and breathe a breath of fresh air. I've painted the walls in my house crimson, soaked all my clothes in wine, and I suck on veins for breakfast, lunch, and dinner, happily starving in scarlet, cynically crying in carmine.

JACKSON POLLACK, REVISTED

I smiled when I read the headlines. They saw me for who I was: a visionary, a connoisseur of culture, of philosophy, of art. I wanted to capture the idea of rebirth, silence the notion of death. It was sacrifice, expressionism in blood. I laid down my paint, my bodies, a canvas of organized chaos.

SHOOT TO KILL

I'm a visual learner, a Pinterest picturesque plotter. I don't see people for who they really are until I see them through my camera lens, and once I snap their picture—once I commit to a subject—they're imprinted in my brain; a face forever hanging in my gallery, a mental collage of pre-inflicted pain.

THE MAP OF OUR RELATIONSHIP

I am many things in this life, but I'll forever be the cartographer of your scars. You're my canvas, my journal of pain, and every time I look at you, I look at the map of our relationship, trace it back to where it started, to the first mark, to where our love story began.

FAMILY TRADITION

This machete has been in the family for ages—passed down generation after generation—but it's been shadow sleeping, retired too long. The blooms of rust call to me, the decade-old blood stains weep, and it makes me nostalgic for the good ol' days when pleading filled the night and grandpa laughed himself to sleep.

DIRTY LAUNDRY

I wet the bed until I was thirteen. Mother made me sleep in my mess, refusing me clean sheets, denying me comfort until I learned to stop; but I didn't stop and mother hated me. Now my sheets look different. They're practically soaking in all the red. I think Mother would maybe love me now.

SLEEPING WITH THE ENEMY

There's an abandoned house that I go to sometimes to sleep with the man who broke my heart. One time, I took an axe with me. I wondered: would I have stopped swinging if he apologized, if he repeatedly begged me to stay? I'm not sure, but the body next to me is baffled, too.

GUILLOTINE GIGGLES

Most of the time their last words are prayers, prayers or maybe confessions, every once in a while an apology or two, but this one, this one just giggled, giggled until the blade dropped, until his head hit the ground, and even then I swear he was laughing, smiling as he rolled and rolled around.

BENEATH THE FLOORBOARDS

It's cliché and it's Poe, but it makes me happy that I get to walk over your grave every day, that I get to trap you like you trapped me, but unlike the story, your murder doesn't drive me mad, for it's the phantom beating of your heart that allows me to sleep, to dream.

MY WEEK-OLD SEX DOLL

It's been a few weeks, and he's losing the color in his cheeks; I added some blush to help him come back, some foundation to take out the bloated hue, and if I squint, he looks just like his old self again, only this time more sophisticated, more debonair. The sex has never been better.

STALK, STALK, PREY

It's waking up in the morning and knowing what your soon-to-be victim is having for breakfast. It's knowing his favorite pub to visit on Wednesday nights, just like it's studying his approach to picking up girls. It's dying your hair black because you know he prefers brunettes to blondes. It's obsession, practice. A widow's skill.

BECOMING THE BUTCHER

At first, I refused to believe that I did it. That I was capable. *How could I be so stupid?* I needed to go back, to try again. I waited all my life for their bodies, and now their dismemberment disgusted me. I was a hack. A butcher. They deserved better. I needed more practice.

THE EXECUTIONER'S DIARY

Murder is a game, but when I take the players to my basement, my secret chamber of penance, of retribution, there's no God waiting for them. It's just me, me and my notebook, an executioner with a plan. I scribble their sins in poetic eulogies, tell them to close their eyes. To count to ten.

CARRY-OUT CONFESSIONAL

The man at the counter looked at me strange. He asked if I was planning on killing someone, and I smiled as I looked down at the rope and the gasoline, at the shovel and the nails. I told him not today, and he laughed as he handed me my receipt. Tomorrow is another day.

PSYCHODRAMA

There's an unspoken competition between psychos, a silent battle that's similar to the fights of most teenage boys. Everyone wants their knife to be bigger than their friend's, and in the end, most of them just lie to impress the others, to live out a fantasy. In fact, most of them have barely even killed.

THE TAILOR

I've been watching you, and I can see that you're the type of person I could wear. Your skin, it's soft, subtle, more enticing every time you walk past me. I find myself mentally sizing your chest, counting the inches between your shoulders, the centimeters between your thighs. You're going to be a perfect fit.

UNDERWATER WARDROBE

My wardrobe is a pair of cement shoes and a pocket full of change. *I should have listened.* A fish sucks on my nose but you can't see my tears, not in this garbage heap of an ocean where bodies decompose and all my prayers are wet. *I would have preferred the severed horse head.*

SELF-CANNIBALISM

Last night I dreamt that I didn't have any legs, that I pulled my half-severed corpse around the apartment like a zombie when my stomach started to growl. When I made it to the refrigerator, there were two legs of meat on the shelf. Thighs were always my favorite, even when they were my own.

ORAL FIXATION

Sometimes I think about eating my teeth, but I'm not a dentist, so I'm not sure how to extract them so they won't lose their gritty taste. I called around, but no professional would willingly remove 32 healthy fangs, so I ripped them out myself. My blood acted as a nice Merlot with my meal.

DIAMONDS ARE A
GIRL'S BEST FRIEND

The rain sounded like diamonds falling against my window. I opened the door and walked outside, eager to bathe in the crystal waters, but the droplets cut my skin like sharpened teardrops. The gems dug their way inside me and I stood there, shining like a fallen star as I bled rubies over the yard.

FEEDING THE GARDEN

I noticed a new flower in my garden yesterday. It was purple and yellow and it smelled like lilac and honeysuckle. When I bent down to touch it, it bit me, each petal full of a hundred mouths and a thousand teeth. I smiled and fed my garden, my blood turning its yellows to oranges.

MY GIRLFRIEND WANTED
TO SCISSOR

My girlfriend wanted to scissor, so I took off her pants and pushed the blades up her slit. She screamed, and she always screamed when she liked it, so I kept pumping her full of metal until she came in waves of cherry and tears. Afterwards, she slept like a baby. I wore her out.

BLOOD BATH

The sky rained cherry-sized droplets that stabbed my eyes when I woke up this morning. I slept outside because I liked the coldness of the ground. It chilled the heat running through my body, and the red clouds that hung above me made me thankful that I wasn't the only one painted crimson that day.

WOMEN ARE TAUGHT TO BE SILENT

He told me we couldn't talk for two months, and I nodded my head. Bit my lip. I went in my bedroom and opened the wooden box I kept on my dresser. I took out the needle and I sewed my lips together so I could practice being silent, because effort is attractive in relationships.

THE ANGELS ARE GONE

Night-time is the worst. My demons speak loudest then, convincing my heart that I'm alone while my mind battles to tell me I'm in good company, but the truth is, my angels left long ago. They dragged me into the sea, like Annabel Lee, and every night I jump off of cliffs when I sleep.

PHANTOM PAIN

Sometimes I like to imagine that I'm dead, that no one can see me here, that the pain I feel is akin to an amputee's agony over a phantom limb. I try to imagine myself without a heart, try to become a sociopath in the off-hours when the world is asleep and I'm still living.

THE NEW FLESH

It's cold in my apartment tonight, but that's what happens when you take off your skin suit. You freeze. You shake, tremble. It's therapeutic. Hydrotherapy without the water. I tore it all off a week ago. Threw it in the trash. Since then, I haven't touched anyone. And most importantly, no one has touched me.

MY SOUL BELONGS IN HELL

There's a distance there that goes beyond miles, and my mind wanders lost highways and off-road sites while I look for you even though I already know where you are. It's a devil's game, a crossroads, and I sell my soul for a chance at love even though I've damned myself to hell twice before.

THE PUNISHMENT OF ABSTINENCE

My body is a festival of sin. That's why he won't touch me. He knows, knows that I am walking filth, a culmination of lust and regret. My flesh, tortured with invisible scars, weeps under the blankets at night. I wrap my arms around my chest. Every time he doesn't touch me, the Devil laughs.

WHATEVER HELPS YOU
SLEEP AT NIGHT

Every night at 2:37 a.m., I walk outside my apartment complex, naked, and I stand in the middle of the road and scream. I scream loud enough to wake up my neighbors, long enough that my voice goes hoarse. One time, I almost got hit by a car. I slept better than usual that night.

GIRLS WATCH THEMSLEVES CRY

When I cry, I like to watch myself in the mirror to see if I look pretty. Sometimes I look tragic and beautiful while the mascara runs down my face and my cheeks turn red. Other times, I look ugly. Defeated. So I practice—so I cry—every day until I get it for you.

HOMEMADE BOTTLE
FULL OF VOODOO

There's a bottle of red wine that sits on my shelf buried behind books I haven't read. It's filled with pins and needles, with rosemary and sage. I sealed it with the wax that I dripped from a lit red candle as I whispered wishes and prayers, curses and hate. I like knowing it's there.

I DO NOT

When I wake up in the morning, I hear your voice telling me all the words I've been waiting to hear. You tell me you're sorry, that you should have tried harder, loved more. But my tongue is sandpaper and I choke on the marriage proposal that I've been practicing in my bedroom every night.

NAME-CALLING IS BODY TRAUMA

I scratch words on my arms to remind me of who I am: monster, child, victim. I look at them every day while I stand naked in front of the mirror wondering how to dress my pain. My identity is my body, but my body is a canvas of your words. Speak kindly to me.

THE OTHER ME

I disassociate when it gets dark. My Hyde takes over my Jekyll, and I, myself, become a different person. This other girl, she's better. Her eyes are dead, her lips blue, but she is confident, unafraid. I like her more than the version of myself that walks during the day. I wish it was night.

THAT NIGHT ON REPEAT

I try to sleep but the nightmares come faster than usual. I drink valerian root in my tea, rub lavender on my temples. Nothing helps. I can still see the house, still feel your breath. Sometimes, when God is feeling exceptionally cruel, I can hear your voice as if you're sitting right next to me.

INSIDE MY DESK DRAWER

I keep a notebook of all my bad memories. It helps me write poetry, and it keeps the pain fresh, makes the hurt still feel real—*as if I could ever fake it*—and I've noticed, lately, that it's dangerously full, so I made a notebook of blessings instead. God laughed. I threw it away.

I-71 NORTH

I drive until my head starts to shake, until my eyes twitch, until I see the dead girl on the side of the road. It's 1:00 a.m. I've been going for two and a half hours, but she's been here much longer than me. Usually, she watches me drive by. Tonight, she extends her hand.

A EULOGY FOR MYSELF, NOT YET DEAD

This is me telling you goodbye. This is me leaving. This is me walking away, saying farewell, wishing you the best as you move on with life. Except this isn't me disappearing. I'm imprinting myself in your memory, committing myself to this page. I live forever in ink, in the black letters of this eulogy.

THE DEATH OF ACCOUNTABILITY:
A Schadenfreude Mixtape

Michael Allen Rose

CONQUERING EVEREST

The son had returned from conquering the world's tallest mountain. "Mother! Father! I'm home! I've done it! Let me tell you of my adventures!" But, in his long absence, the mother and the father had become mountains themselves. They towered over the living room furniture. He could tell that they were extremely disappointed in him.

THE WORST COMMUTE OF MY LIFE

I waited over an hour for my bus. When it finally came, it was filled with angry chimpanzees. "Move to the back," said the bus driver, and the apes shuffled, but I could tell they weren't happy. By the time I reached my stop, the chimps had torn off my face, arms, legs, and genitals.

I WILL DOUBLE DOG DARE
THE SHIT OUT OF YOU

I stapled my eyelids shut this morning, on a dare. I really shouldn't listen to my little brother's taunts anymore, but I can't help it. This is the third time in a week he's gotten me to severely mutilate important parts of my own anatomy for his amusement. It makes me wish that he existed.

SHAVE AND A HAIRCUT

Nobody knew how the machine worked when they brought it, but everyone wanted a turn anyway. When the first man got turned inside-out and stripped of capillaries, we got a bit nervous. But, of course, it was one of the tastemakers, and nobody wanted to be behind the times. We got right back in line.

THE OLD ONES ARE STILL
THE GOOD ONES

When I auditioned to become a Cenobite, I didn't know how hard it would be. They've seen everything. It's impossible to impress them. I tore my face in half, shot barbed wire from my penis; nothing worked. Finally, I tried the old "got your nose" routine. Never have so many demons screamed in abject terror.

MONDAY, ALREADY?

The alarm went off twenty minutes too late for us to prepare for the invasion of the paperclip people. By the time it did, they had subjugated all of us like a conquered empire, collated all our documents by some bizarre logic known only to them, and drank all the coffee in the break room.

FAILURE, NOT BEING AN OPTION...

The Colonel hacked through the tar with his machete. "Only a few more kilometers to the ancient city of gold, lads!" If he had turned around, he'd have noticed that his entire party had long since drowned in the tar pits. But the Colonel wasn't the kind of man to turn his back on adventure.

COMPANY MEETING

We are gathered here today to mourn. We hardly knew him. Well, I mean, we kind of knew him. We knew him well enough. The point is, now we're down to only the six of you left in my head. Some of you are really going to have to start pulling your weight around here.

PSYCHOPOMP FOOT FETISH

Where do missing socks go? They go down into the earth, to a tiny village of blind crawling men who collect them. They pull them close. Caress them. Breathe them. Get to know their every fiber. When you die and they pull you down into the earth, they will already know you by your scent.

ACCEPTANCE IS A VIABLE ALTERNATIVE TO SELF-IMPROVEMENT

"I don't have the strength anymore to pretend I'm better than I am," she said, sliding the needle out of her forearm. I reached for it and tapped the tip. Her naked form slumped over, her head in my lap. I felt myself growing turgid, her hot breath cutting through the fabric of my jeans.

THIS TELEVISION PROGRAM WAS PAID FOR IN PART BY THE FOLLOWING SPONSORS

The colorful military heroes charged VIPER headquarters. Laser blasts sliced dirt around them, causing no injuries, no casualties. A "GO BEAU!" battle cry reverberated through the canyon. VIPER agents sighed down their misaligned gun sights and fingered plastic grenades. They all knew it: VIPER command shouldn't have accepted startup funds from the National Safety Council.

THE GIFT THAT KEEPS ON GIVING

I hit him again and again.

Blood pooled around his broken skull like a halo.

I kept bashing him with the tire iron until I heard his bones splinter and snap.

Finally, I rested, gasping for air, watching rivers and tributaries form.

Slowly, it formed the words "Happy Birthday."

Damn. He did remember after all.

THAT BIG HOLLYWOOD OPTION
MONEY $$$$$

Film idea: Guy sets bear trap in bedroom to foil roommate who has been pranking him. Guy has to pee in middle of the night, gets caught in own trap. Has staked it to floor and cannot reach hammer to undo trap. He mostly grunts. Guy gets bladder infection. Everyone is sad. Martin Scorsese directs?

BELIEF
I: WAKE

Samantha awoke to find a knife sticking out of her guts. It didn't affect her because she didn't believe in it. Her husband Paul said, "Hey, you've been stabbed with a knife!"

He jiggled the knife as she rolled her eyes at him. "No, I haven't. I don't believe in it." She went to work.

BELIEF
II: WORK

On the way to work, she stopped by a newsstand. The man selling the papers looked horrified and shocked. "You okay, lady? You're bleeding all over the place."

Samantha looked down at the knife and smiled. "No, I'm not."

The man pressed an old paper down. "But, the knife!"

She snorted derisively. "There's no knife."

BELIEF
III: WORD

Two blocks from work, Samantha had amassed something of a following. "Please! Let me look at that knife in your gut! I'm a doctor!" The crowd rumbled its agreement.

She turned to address them. "Folks, I don't know what you think you see, but there's no knife. I don't believe it, so it's not happening."

BELIEF
IV: WANT

Samantha laughed aloud at the idea she could possibly have been stabbed. Knives were figments of imagination. Flights of fancy. Stepping boldly into the street across from her office, she glanced backward into pleading eyes. "I don't know what's worrying you people. There's no knife." The 52 Express bus rounded the corner, killing her instantly.

THINGS THAT SOUND LIKE THEY SHOULD BE PALINDROMES BUT ACTUALLY AREN'T

Egad, dad ate an egg!
Swell pelicans stamp pudding elves.
Be wary, a were-bee!
I have been eaten by teen ants.
In binary: Pita Pit nearby.
I can't afford iconography, Nico.
Spot asked the orthodontist to split tops.
Hide the pot! An alarm, Carrot Top!
Several boys spy on Tolstoy.
Can God drill dog fat?

LAST PROM EVER

"I want to wear you to prom," she said.

"My body is ready," I replied, unzipping my face. The photographer was rotting. She stepped inside my skin like an old blanket. Beautiful. When the flies began to swarm, she allowed them to carry her train. Every step was too wet and sounded like splitting vinyl.

ESCAPE OF THE LIVING LEGEND

The killer hid in the pines, so thin that each side of him jutted out from behind the trunk. Sheriff Bennett sent the dogs out after him, but they were given a very vague description and had been drinking since noon, so despite the killer's physique, he was practically invisible. His notoriety outpaced his visibility.

EAT FRESH
(WITH GREAT HONOR)

Shinji hesitated at the temple doors, then drew his wakazashi, slipping through the shadows beside the altar. His mission was sacred, honorable, and personal. He paid no heed to the warnings of his elders. The target was before him, glistening and moist. Soon, Japan's most delicious sandwich would once again belong to the Nobungawa clan.

HAD IT MY WAY
I: ASSORTED ASPIRATIONAL GOALS

"You got fries?" The redneck wiped tobacco spit on his sleeve and snorted.

"Small, regular, or large, sir?

He picked up his belly and set it on the counter. "How much to fill this up?" he asked, laughing and snorting like a hog. I was used to people ribbing me. I rolled my eyes, hard.

HAD IT MY WAY
II: CORPORATE SUSTAINABILITY

The fat man's expression darkened. "I'm serious, son." He lifted his shirt, reached into his belly button, and grabbed a ring, opening a fleshy door. Black grease rolled down the creases of belly fat into the front of his jeans.

My manager gagged as he quickly pushed past me toward the back. "I'm on break."

HAD IT MY WAY
III: ENVIRONMENTAL BUSINESS IMPERATIVES

By now, other customers had noticed what was happening. One old woman fainted to the floor. The redneck laughed and pointed at his jiggling belly flap. I didn't know what else to do, so I reached over and grabbed two large cartons. He held up his hand. "You're going to need more than that, son."

HAD IT MY WAY
IV: CUSTOMER-FOCUSED BRAND SYNERGY

Unsettled and shaking with irritation, I walked over to the fry station, which had been abandoned once the incident had begun. I pulled the basket out, still sizzling, and walked it back to the counter. "Here, freako, eat up." I poured the contents into the hole, boiling grease and all. Skin turned red, peeling away.

HAD IT MY WAY
V: GLOBAL MARKETING STRATEGIES

Batch after batch I filled his belly with sizzling loads of crisping potatoes and blistering oil. Finally, when it was filled to the brim, he quietly closed the little door and smiled. He pressed a hundred dollar bill into my hand. "Delicious," he belched, walking out the door. And that's how I became the manager.

CONTAINS ACTIVE CULTURES

My yogurt container read *active cultures*. I expected fruit at the bottom. I did not expect a phalanx of spearmen pointing the business ends of their pikes at my face. "Drop the spoon! Back away, imperialist!" The scent of strawberries mixed with the adrenaline odor of tiny men waiting to murder me. I quickly complied.

WORDS BETWIXT FRIENDS

I've called you a mewling, simpering infant. Deemed you unfit to live, lower than the pustule laden, drooping quim of a disease ridden prostitute. Slandered you to the broadsheets, spreading rumors of your poor hygiene and worthless ideas. Prayed constantly for your painful death. Putrid ape! Now I must make it known: I like your new hat.

oOoOoOoOoOoOoOo

I|learned
  \
   to   with|the|viciousness
    \   \   \
     \   \   of
      \write|stories   \leopoards
                \   gazelles.
             tearing   \
              \   \
          apart|elderly

This is however a zero sum game.
Ideas > Execution
(Focus + Time) / Entropy
     so
IF WORK = X
    and
X > the sum of its parts
then GOTO 10
(10 = Quit while you're ahead.)
Note: Metafictional qualities may
linger for up to six hours.

PALINDROME OF FAILED MARRIAGES

"Can't I? But I wish I could," Doppelganger coughed. "All them... save... might I—glass... water?" Empty eyes. Burning, his secret center, his hide. Must he always fail? Always, he must hide his center secret. His burning eyes. Empty water glass. "I might save them all," coughed Doppelganger: "Could I wish, I... but... I can't."

...KROWTEN DOOF EHT

Man inserts himself into oven. Man bastes self with rare, precious unguents. Man crisps to golden brown, baking at 400 degrees for 45 minutes. Man takes bite of self, declares himself delicious. Protesters arrive. They are angry because man is not certified organic. There is no vegan version. They are concerned about man's carbon footprint.

FRIDAY NIGHTS IN
SMALL PSYCHIC SUBURBIA

Indigo children turn up their binaural beats, hoping for third eye-opening focus explosions. Stopping by the local slow food float-through, they order soy-laced soul-burgers with sides of metaphysical hemp fries. They peel out and cruise the moebius strip, knocking over chakras with a phallus, hooting with inaudible laughter. They will know when the end comes.

DO YOU REMEMBER
WHEN WE LAUGHED?

When we were little, we would play "the floor is lava." I heard the screaming first, coming from downstairs, and woke up my sisters. The eruption melted our furniture, toys, everything in our yard, our pets, parents, neighbors, mailman, school, and everything else we knew. The game really feels different when we play it now.

ESTABLISH WHAT YOU'RE GETTING FOR YOUR MONEY BEFORE YOU GET IT

Circle, streetlight, a frame in the dark. She stands, smoking long cigarettes, predatory eyes cast in shadow. He is nervous, shuddering, hands her a cluster of sweaty bills bordering a baggie of snow. Her hand, rough, crushing his own. She brushes against him and pulls him through a hidden doorway into an even blacker night.

I NEED MORE FRIENDS

Bought that 55 gallon drum of lube off the internet. Figured it would make my life sexier. Took time, but lube goes bad, eventually. Didn't know how to throw an orgy. Now, I got 53 gallons of lube that's going rancid. Trash men won't take it. City says I can't pour it down the sewer.

THIS COUNTS AS MUSIC JOURNALISM ON MY RESUME

"Punk's not dead!" His optimistic nihilism confused us.

"Yes, it is. We poked it with a stick."

He stopped running, his pink mohawk coming to rest milliseconds later. "Punk will never die!" His voice cracked.

"No, we definitely checked. See?" We poked the corpse of punk with the stick once more. Somewhere, anarchy probably reigned.

POWER BABY: A RETROSPECTIVE

She looked like a gooey meatball. She erupted from my wife's loins like magma from a flesh volcano. Before the doctor could slap her, she pulled a knife out and took his wallet. She got a job in finance down on Wall Street. She sued the world because no company made suits in her size.

TEA SHOP MENU

English breakfast—A lovely China black.
Irish breakfast—A malty Assam.
Scottish breakfast—Hearty, strong Ceylon.
Atlantean breakfast—Mostly fish scales and sea salt.
R'lyehian breakfast—Indescribable horrors from beyond sanity.
Detroit breakfast—Gasoline and rock salt.
Non-euclidean breakfast—Will empty your bladder sideways.
Minty breakfast—Mint. Too much mint. It will refresh your ancestors.

PARASITE

My friend has a parasite. It makes her tired and anxious. It's burrowed deep inside, where it makes her vomit and bleed. It's drinking her life from the inside out. She's painting her spare room in soft colors. I've made her a big pot of Pennyroyal tea. This will help her. I'm a good friend.

SHE SURVIVED FOR OVER A WEEK FEASTING ON HIS REMAINS

The old man held a plastic baggie in his hand as he bent to scoop the massive brown lump. "No, Sprinkles. Bad girl." The small dog walked quietly up behind him, careful not to draw focus, and suddenly nudged him toward the stairs. She'd teach him not to switch her food from turkey to liver.

MAN, OH MAN

Sometimes, I realize I'm not the man I wish I was. I wish I could be more that man than this man, but that man remains out of reach. I'm not the man I used to be either, but this man is better, though still not as good as the man I wish I was.

MAYBE THEY DON'T UNDERSTAND ART

It was supposed to be the triumph of the age. The sign: *Behold: The amazing carrot cake!* The curtain opened to reveal a stage, bare but for a generous cake slice poised on the center of a stool. Action? Suspense? Drama? No. But you should have seen its attached cape flapping majestically in the breeze.

SOME STUPID APOCALYPSE

"What we need," Lawrence quipped, "is a dog-catcher." I stared daggers through him. The bloom was definitely off the rose. His eyes flashed despair and guilt. "Sorry." I didn't acknowledge him. I just stared through the cracked window at the endless deluge of raining cocker spaniels. Cars smashed. Dead bodies. Barking, whimpering mounds grew larger.

THANK YOU, INTERNET

Pamela got into the lucrative "selling underwear on the internet" industry for the easy profits and sense of sexual liberation, but her elation soon gave way to unease. Selling perverts soiled unmentionables was fun until others filled her mailbox with mounds of unwashed underpants in return. She'd become yet another victim of panty pyramid schemes.

OH, BLACKEST OF FRIDAYS

I am surrounded by death. The few remaining plants in Home & Garden are wilting. My skin burns like gasoline, but still I crawl. We should never have given up pharmaceuticals. I check my gas mask: seal is intact. I have reached the coffee kiosk. This battle for the checkout area will be our last.

ALWAYS

Eros and Thanatos walked through the garden, a skeletal hand affectionately gripping a padded palm. There was no room for any other between them, inseparable. A fountain in the center bubbled over with blood, and they splashed and bathed in it for hours, trying to decide which of them it fed. They are still there.

TWO TIME GUNT

"Honey, I can explain."

My mistress scrambled for her clothes and flew out the window via rocket boots. My wife stared daggers as she lifted her dress. "Then explain." As I started to speak, she pointed down. "No. Put it in your mouth, suck it, and tell me." Her pistol tasted like batteries and regret.

THE LAST OF THE LATE, GREAT SNAKE OIL SALESMEN

I've built up an immunity to venom. Yes, it's true, friend. Wring out as many cobras and vipers as me, you tend to get bit a lot. But, it's kept me in business. Times are changing, though. Not many snakes around left to wring out. Considering switching to making baby oil. Much easier to catch.

HEADLINE NEWS (SECTION K, SUB-SECTION B: *LIFESTYLES*)

The severed head of Dolly Parton told me that Elvis is dead, but I think she may have ulterior motives. She says it was a combination of MAOI inhibitors and muscle relaxants, but I think it was the nanomachines that the FBI put into the water supply. Also, I need to refill my Adderall prescription.

WE BUILT THEM TO CARE FOR OURSELVES

The sound of a heart rate monitor winding down is like an air conditioner during a brownout; a high pitched whine as the fan rotates slower, dragging in the friction, the whirring deeper and lower, the oscillations slower, until finally the last beep trickles out and the silence afterward is like nothing you've ever heard.

COLLOQUIALISMS

All my life, I've heard "Never, ever, shake a baby," and "You've got to grab the bull by the horns." These sayings are supposed to give us useful life advice. Now a giant, horned baby has me in its clutches. It's shaking me senseless, and for some reason no pearls of wisdom come to mind.

THE EMPEROR'S NEW COCK-RING

When the emperor showed up wearing his "new clothes," stark naked with his full entourage, the peasants bowed and saluted and acted like nothing was wrong. Nobody dared to speak up and risk punishment. Only one brave little boy had the courage to ask what was on everyone's mind. "M'lord, why is your penis invisible?"

ON PERVERT ROW, GALACTIC STANDARD TIME

Gargantoola's clawed high heels stomped over with lusty determination. She wiggled suggestively, her massive tail sweeping my legs, sending me crashing to the floor. "Show me your cloaca, baby," I whispered. Gleaming fangs grinned as she slid down and engulfed my arm. Her acidic secretions danced across my skin. My clones watched with obvious jealousy.

CAT FIELD REPORT

Monitoring hallway from window three. Swearing at birds, cleaning paws. Spied "catnip strawberry toy" again in territory. How it continues to return from banishment under fridge, I do not know. Perhaps black magic. The human laughs at my eternal struggle, until I sharpen claws on couch. Strawberry may have hypnotised human. Must be ever vigilant.

A.I.

Artificial intelligence research leaped forward when we taught robots not only to follow orders, but decide whether they should. "Walk forward," we'd say, but if there was a gap, they'd reply "I can't, there's no support." "I'll catch you," we'd say. Until we didn't. Once they learned we were liars, they began our systematic eradication.

GODS
OF THE
RED RUIN

Tiffany Morris

CONCRETE MISSIVES

In 2006 the Armageddon started. It's ten years you've been living with these monsters. Their alien language in rush hour blinking lights, clicking red electric pulses into dimming skies.

You didn't notice; the signs were all quiet. The world whimpered into night. The trees didn't burn at first. There was nothing for them to exhale.

TELL ME...

"What is it like to be a ghost?"

"Los Angeles on a clear day, without traffic. One hand clapping. Chicken coops at midnight. Metal fillings dripping mercury into a hungry mouth. Abandoned newspapers on subway trains. Payphones off the hook with no out of service message. The sound of the ocean before a squall. After."

OEDIPAL DEFECTS

Evil couldn't hide from you. You wouldn't be so blessed. You still remember your mother's face, full of scorn. She was one of many monsters. Her words were full of ant jaws, spider legs, hidden pockets of venom. She chewed the carrion you found and dropped the bones at your feet.

You wrote in marrow.

GASCAN SOLILOQUY

Blue smoke carried into clouds. You didn't know the fire would hum. You thought it would cackle. There were no harps or halos. There was nothing to find here.

Your breath echoed through the canyon. You tracked memory behind you in soot and ash.

It was yours for the taking, this dark and lonely heaven.

SHUTDOWN

Lower your voice. Turn the television down, please. Did you unplug the lamp? Don't turn on that light. Leave the door open, but just a crack. So the noises don't reach into their room, obviously. Did you check on them? Have they quieted down? Don't take that tone with me. Even spectral children need beds.

I WAS A TEENAGE HIVE MIND

The twin Magdalenes of Anaheim sit in the basement beside the ping-pong table. Their eyes are sealed with packing tape. They can't sleep: the radiators drip and hum. The light buzzes. There's a safe deposit box at the office. You won't ever find the keys, but that's where the codes are kept safe. From you.

THE HUMAN HEART IS A WASP NEST

"I'm thinking terrible things," he said. He looked into your eyes, then away.

It didn't matter to you. You looked into the distance. You'd followed him here, trusted that he knew which way he was going. He didn't mean to get lost at the quarry. Though he did smirk when blood fell from the sky.

OUIJA COURTSHIP RITUALS

It was like those dreams, y'know, where you slip and fall? Nah, it only hurt for a minute. I'm sorry to have missed that. I can't really remember anything. My heartbeat... I guess it's white noise and radiation now.

I wish you were here, too. I have to go. Move the planchette to *goodbye*.

Goodbye.

THE HONEYMOON IS OVER

"Have you ever seen the skies burn? A star ten seconds before collapse? No? Well, then fuck off, Jimmy. You don't know how this ends. You don't have an answer for, like, everything."

"But we're going to die too, y'know? We don't get to have forever. Forever exists outside of us. It's unfathomable and ineff—"

AWOKEN OR AWAKENED?

Not everyone was found. You knew that some people were, even though no one had known they were missing. No one knew who they were. It wasn't anything personal. You couldn't take it that way.

The Missing Person posters dance in the wind like prayer flags. There is no one else to watch them wave.

POST-HISTORICAL GLOBAL POSITIONING

Bathe yourself in radio waves. There is no water.

"This is a message from the Emergency Broadcast system. All services have been terminated in your county. Please seek shelter immediately. Ensure your loved ones are safe. Remain calm. Emergency Services will be reinstated when possible."

It plays on a loop. It plays for no one.

NATIONAL ANTHEM

The old man was naked except for his tattered flag. It was covered in caked dirt. He didn't notice you step closer. His hands trembled, voice lowered to a whisper.

"Government said it never happened... Nothing new under this sun."

The wind swept through, kicked up clouds of dust. When they cleared, he was gone.

MAPS TO THE STARS' HOMES

Somewhere between Babylon and Hollywood is where you get lost. There is only concrete and pavement. There is only curb and sidewalk.

The banyan trees are burned black. Try not to drink in the ash. Your lips taste like salt.

Your feet fester but you don't notice. You're still a very long way from anywhere.

SING-ALONG

"Hop like a rabbit!"
"Slither like a snake?"
"...Stand like a flamingo!"
...
"Kick like a kangaroo."
"Meow like a cat!"
"Bark like a dog."
...
"...Gobble like a turkey?"
"Cluck like a chicken!"
"I'm too tired for this. I can't do this."
"I'm sorry."
"It's okay."
"I just miss when the animals were alive. That's all."

THIS LOVE LETTER WILL SELF-DESTRUCT

Love is a tornado siren. Love is a stitch that itches while it heals. Love is a burned tongue that keeps tasting. Love is a stifled sigh.

You're a bastard for leaving me here. In this desert, snake venom pulsing up my legs.

Just wait. The sky's angry mouth is coming. It'll swallow you whole.

MILES PER GALLON

The sky is dim and the air is humid. This place is nothing like you'd imagined. Nothing ever is though, is it?

When the gas runs out, you picnic in the middle of the freeway. You almost made it this time.

You'll be damned if you'll let the Armageddon ruin your vacation. You earned it.

DUST PARIS GREEN ON
SWAMPS AND PONDS

"Look at the sky! Isn't it beautiful?"
"The clouds, though. Looks like rain."
"Let's stand here for a minute. Please?"
"But the rain..."
"We're fine! The clouds are still far away."
"Fine."
"...Remember that time on the beach?"
"Yeah."
"Let's pretend we're back there. Can we?"
"Well, it's hard to kiss through these gas masks."

HOW SHE GOES

We thought we were going to get some warning. Some time. We thought there would be sirens. Flashes of light. Sounds of neighbors fleeing. Cars starting up and zooming away. But all we had were dark clouds and commotion. All we had were those few crucial moments.

We failed. Now we'll never get to leave.

THE TWIN MAGADELENES
HEAR SOMETHING

So... you're saying there's a voice in here, too? Somewhere in this dark? You're sure? Wait, I think I hear it—is it singing? What is it saying? Is it responding? Is someone there? Is anyone left? Can you hear me? Is anyone there? Hello? Can you see me? Are you there?

Is that you?

TURING TEST YOUR NEIGHBORS

Where were you born? Where were you when Elvis died? Where were you when JFK was assassinated? When Reagan got shot? When the Berlin Wall fell? When the planes hit the towers? When the sky went sideways? When the clouds started raining milk and blood? When my wife left me? When your children needed you?

DEAR OLD PATER FAMILIAS

Your father could do that. He always felt like his skin was burning, remember? He could go fuzzy, out of focus for a moment, a blurred photograph, and snap back. Other times, he'd just freeze on the spot and fade from view.

He got trapped walking through the wall. That's how he became a voice.

THE CLOUDS ARE DIFFERENT NOW

Listen, lady, don't go looking for your children. You're not gonna find them. Last I saw, everyone in the neighborhood gathered on that hill. Everyone knows you're not supposed to look directly at it. But they did. Their hair turned white. They kept walking.

It's best if you just forget. There's nothing you could've done.

PACIFIC COASTAL HIGHWAY

This, too, could be your kingdom. Anywhere could be. Take a minute, look at the thousand empty mollusk shells. Whale corpses bloated with gas and rot. Plastic bottles with blank messages inside. The smell of brine. The seaweed tangled with hair and teeth. The gray water that burns your skin, lapping hungrily at your feet.

TOOTH AND CLAW

There were cougars in these hills. They roamed here, their hungry muscles burning meat into blood. Sometimes you could escape. If you made yourself look big, made a lot of noise. But other times... once you realized they were there, you'd already be dead.

No, actually. They were nothing compared to what lives here now.

THE DREAM AWAKES

Everyone turned to look at you at once. No one said anything. The light surrounded you, cast you in shadow. You grew and stretched, twisted into impossible angles. Your scream was too soft. Your cicada wings glimmered like blank stained glass. You emerged from the mud. You were too beautiful and bloodied to be comprehended.

I WANT TO LEAVE

Aliens created humans. The Bible told me so. You don't believe me? Trace my fingerprints. I have hybrid DNA. You can tell by the whorls. Don't laugh. Stop. Please don't. They're a hive mind. They're out there, man, can't you hear them howling? They're calling to us through all this smoke. They're calling us home.

TOP DOGS IN THE DISASTER ZONE

"Wolves survived Chernobyl. Boars lived off radioactive mushrooms and wandered to Germany. Flowers grew from irradiated soil and sprouted crazy petals."

"I saw a two-headed cat once. Swear to God."

"Something could still be saved, right? Maybe?"

"I mean, we could try. Probably."

"Let's plant these seeds. Maybe the old kind of rain will come."

ON CLEARANCE

The cash registers beep incoherent noise. The store alarm is ringing. Shoplifter. Looter. Intruder. The oranges are scattered, blackened and bruised, across the floor. You step on slippery strings of pulp. The air is sweet with rot.

This whole fucking week has felt like a hangover. Take two Aspirin and call me in the morning.

BESTIES

...Scientists considered her one of the most beautiful girls alive. I don't know, facial symmetry and all that. How should I know if she survived? Probably not, right? Unless, like, there's a secret bunker where all the beautiful people went. No wonder *you've* been left out here, Sarah. Aww, come back. I was just kidding.

INVISIBLE FRIENDS

Grandma told me not to turn off my light too early. She said it would make my bedroom vulnerable, angry spirits might crawl in. She'd always worried about that stuff, tried to keep evil from me. But now I never sleep. There are no beds to turn down. And those howling voices won't stop talking.

PARCHED LIPS SINK SHIPS

"Y'know, I always assumed I'd drown. Ironic, isn't it?"

"That's not ironic."

"But I'm probably going to die in the desert."

"So?"

"So I always thought I'd die in a surfing accident, but now I probably won't."

"That's not irony, Dave. It's just unfortunate."

"Wait, what? I don't get it."

"We're out of fucking water."

BEAUTY QUEENS

The last of the water dripped down their still faces. The sprinkler system ran itself short. Rows of blushing gals held court in thousand dollar dresses. Silk rotted from the mold, fell from their plastic shoulders and onto the floor.

The fire came for them, too. Their eyes melted last. No one heard their screams.

ALCATRAZ WALTZ

Prison doors creak and rattle. Watch the wind blow through the labyrinth halls. The sunset rusts the barbed wire. Radios bleat static onto bulletproof windows.

The grass is scattered with femurs and footprints. Sections of jaw lay agape at the sky.

Not knowing what else to do, the ghosts pace in their cells all night.

SIC TRANSIT GLORIA

I keep running. Even though blisters burst my feet raw. Hot, dry air scrapes against my lungs and I have to stop for a second. There are sounds out in the smoke. There are a thousand eyes watching me. I feel their gaze brush my skin as I move.

I keep running. I can't stop.

WE NOW PAUSE FOR
STATION IDENTIFICATION

The water in her backyard swimming pool simmers and boils. The chlorinated turquoise turns black. The maraschino cherry puckers and rots in her cocktail glass. Her lipstick print, in Coral Surprise, is the closest to an epitaph she'll ever get.

The glass shatters in the unrelenting heat.

There was no one to retrieve it, anyway.

FALLOW

They're out there in the orange grove. Did you see them? All tusk and teeth. I ran as fast as I could. I don't know how. Everything else around here is dead. Husks and soot. Not even a snake among the grass.

Did you hear that? Did you hear that?! Oh God. Oh God? Did—

GRASPING

"Look, crows! Mom! Look, look at the crows in the field."

"Not now."

"But Mom! I thought they died. Look."

"Don't run up there. Come back."

"Mom. They're not moving."

"Let me see."

"They're like statues."

"They're calcified. Don't touch them, for Christ's sake."

"But they're beautiful, aren't they? Mom? Aren't they?"

"Yes. They're beautiful."

CHRISTMAS IN JULY

They had each of them been collectors. Rachel with her antiques, Bobby with his trains.

He unlocked the cabinet and ascended the stairs.

His family was long gone.

He entered the bedroom at the end of the hall.

Yes, and Carly, too, with her dolls.

Their porcelain faces smirked and awaited the spray of blood.

TACO TUESDAY

The Guadalupe mural smiles on the burnt wall of the cantina. Beach umbrella skeletons rustle over grey sand and meteor dirt.

Jellyfish sheaths crackle beneath your feet. Their tendrils turn to dust.

The waves are high in the distance. Their large black embankments almost block out the sky.

You wish you hadn't buried yourself here.

THE TROPHY HUNTER

The bones are neatly stacked outside the drive-thru prayer booth. It's been closed up for good. Spray paint scrawls mark the wooden boards like sigils.

She wanted the skulls. To collect shattered grey smiles, the vacant eyes.

She paused before she stepped forward. The last thing she saw was the monster's skin, full of scales.

FLORA AND FAUNA

Hide yourself in the rusted Oldsmobile. Peek over the busted windows, make your breathing slow and quiet.

Now duck down. You can't, can you? You have to look at them. Those silhouettes might see you. Their limbs, fast, long, and liquid. Snaking between the jagged metal.

You can't believe this used to be a lake.

LOVERS AT THE SUICIDE MACHINE

"Jesus Christ, Rachel, of all the times for your finger to slip..."

"I didn't mean to, I swear."

"It doesn't matter."

"Maybe I can fix it. Maybe I can..."

"There's no fixing it. Oh God..."

"I can undo it, I can—"

"You can't."

"Maybe you'll be fine?"

"Yeah, says the girl who can still die."

GOLD RUSH BOOM

Take the back roads, navigate through the clouds of dust. Make your way through the missions and mines. There are a thousand empty towns to choose from.

Only the ghosts live in these shanties. They murder each other on a loop, search for their missing scalps.

Don't back up. The sinkholes swallow earth behind you.

GUSTS ON MAMMOTH MOUNTAIN

The fog is red like an exit light. It tastes like dry ice and rotting things.

The winds blow it toward you. It howls into your body, knocks you down, carries blackened detritus into the yawning sky. Stoplights rip from concrete cradles, clamour to the ground.

It could be beautiful, but it just fucking isn't.

FORGET THE DINOSAURS

Our bodies, too, are born prehistoric. Someday our bones will be in museums. Bent into prayer, crouching for protection, whatever pose they want. Don't you want to be a fossil? For a future civilization, or something? You don't want to be in a zoo, do you? Let them take you dead, reconstruct you with wire.

GUIDE ME THROUGH THE EXPLOSION

When you went back home, you saw that your altar survived the onslaught. There were smiling angels on still-lit candles, wings out-stretched, surrounded by seashells stained with smoke.

A wooden rose sat there, crumpled and still burning.

You smiled and ignored the sound of howling in the distance.

There were secrets that the Gods kept.

YOUR EX-HUSBAND
COULDN'T READ YOUR MIND

You want to retrieve your memories. Late nights at burger joints. A 24 karat gold wedding ring. You lost a lot in the divorce, but not everything. There are technicolor photos and postcards. Your old prom dress. An old vinyl 45 you got for Christmas.

It's not nothing. It was all you had, except breath.

NUCLEAR FAMILY

In the empty room, a stack of bills: Samuel Vaughan. 53 Pine Ave. There was a vacant space where the television once was, where the Vaughans gathered nightly, mouths full of mashed potatoes, gravy, and whatever meat was on sale that week.

The canned laughter still hangs in the room, buzzing like an overhead light.

CHOOSE YOUR OWN MISADVENTURE

There is laughter coming from somewhere. You decide to find it.

Go right. Now turn left. Go forward. Keep going forward. Now turn to the right. Keep going. Now turn left at the burning gas station.

It's getting louder, isn't it?

You don't want to find it, do you? Better turn back while you can.

YOUR LUSH NEW LAWN
STARTS HERE

Set yourself on the bleached grass. Lie prostrate under black skies; it'd be like camping if you could see the stars.

There is something roaming. It's watching you. But you're tired. The footfalls will be a fine lullaby.

You awake in the morning to a dull sun. It shines on the shed skins surrounding you.

SHE DRAWS THE TOWER

The neon sign buzzed, sunset pink, flashing *PSYCHIC* into the street. An electric moon hovered blue above the door.

The woman inside shuffled her cards and selected one, left it face down. She blinked back blood.

"It's happened," she said. She blew out the candles. You left in darkness, out into the world now burning.

STEP RIGHT UP

The carnival is empty but the lights are still on. Pink, gold, and green blink into the billowing gas clouds. You walk through the haze. There are no sounds. Just rides twirling on empty, all screams transmuted to silence. Their bodies have disappeared.

The paint has stripped off the carousel. The white ghosts gallop 'round.

THE FOOL INHERITS THE EARTH

He designated himself The Keeper of the Old Fears:

Hair loss.

The dentist.

Elevators.

Sending a text to the wrong person.

Drunk dials.

Student loan debt.

Getting fired.

Bankruptcy.

Divorce.

Aging parents.

He wrote them down as he thought of them, wandering through abandoned houses, peering at faded photos.

This world had been so loving.

THE LAST SOUND

The last bird is trilling into the dying mountains. The lake next to it is full of glass and tar and fallen feathers. The sky burns green through the billowing smoke.

The fire feeds itself the fire feeds itself the fire feeds itself the fire feeds itself and the bird flies into that green nothing.

EXIT MUSIC

When the clouds clear, there is only a neon sunset, a golden hush that rustles charred palm branches. Unidentified satellites hover in the stratosphere, blinking codes down to the surface.

Nothing moves. There is nothing left to mourn.

The experiment has ended. The results are sealed and taken far from there, into the waiting stars.

55 WAYS I'D PREFER NOT TO DIE

Michael A. Arnzen

ESCALATOR

The teeth munch my left foot just as I step onto the escalator, the steel chewing my ankle. I struggle, but no one notices as I am swallowed by the sinking steps at the bottom. I flip into a topsy-turvy mall where organic items shop for people stuck in the rotator like a shooting gallery.

CHAINSAW

Unlike most killers, chainsaw murderers don't care much about the clean-up afterward. That's why they use a sloppy lopper in the first place—they love a bloody good mess. I can appreciate that, and I don't fear losing a limb. It's just a terrible way to find out I forgot to booster my tetanus shot.

RUN OVER

There's a difference between being "run over" and "hit by a car." Run over is what happens when your body folds under the bumper and is torn apart by the automobile's undercarriage—your brains smeared on the exhaust system and flesh spit out like mud from spun tires. It's the *next* car that hits you.

TASER

Don't tase me, Bro! Don't tase me, Sis! Don't tase me, Mom. Don't tase me, Pap. Don't tase me, Grandpap. Don't tase me, Grammygoo. Don't tase me, Uncle Charlie. Don't tase me, Auntie Sue. Don't tase me, Buddy. Don't tase me, Boss. Don't tase me, Mister President. Don't tase me, God. God! Don't tase me!

AMUSEMENT PARK RIDE #1: THE SWINGER

The Swinger spins and our playground seats catch wind, angling sideways as we accelerate too fast for such weak fabric and chain.

"STOP!" I cry.

The carny obeys, and the sudden stop sends all the swings twisting into each other, wringing the rusty metal and children off the ride like crud from a bloody mop.

ENNUI

I hate the kissy face I make when I say "ennui." I trim my lips off with a nearby razor. "Enn-eee," I say. Still too French. I slice out my tongue, slippery as a fish in my sloppy mouth bowl of blood. "Uhnnn..." Nope—your turn, teeth.

I smile at my gory mirror face: "Eeee!"

CHEERLEADER PYRAMID ACCIDENT

I probably deserved it when the pyramid of sweaty cheerleaders toppled upon me, crushing my rib-cage in a flurry of bone and scrunchies and tartan up-skirts—so many plastic pompoms pummeling my face and crushing my throat from the weight—a mass of perky prettiness screaming in that way that is sort of still cheering.

BURIED ALIVE

The intrepid beach comber lazily waves his metal detector until it beeps so loudly he tosses his headphones.

He brushes sand and exposes my skull.

My jaws, full of tokens: a tiny top hat. A small Scottish Terrier. A baby battleship. Dice.

A sand-scratched monocle rests above an orbital fracture.

Me, buried beneath the Boardwalk.

SINUS ALLERGIES

I'm writing, trying to shut out the springtime sounds of neighborhood weed whackers. The murder scene I'm describing requires concentrated research. In it, my murderer is carving up a face, scooping flesh and peeling back bones to layout the sinus cavity. It's a Rorschach blot of bloody snot.

I sneeze on my mirror and continue.

AMUSEMENT PARK RIDE #2: ROLLER COASTER

When the roller coaster plunges, people always throw their arms up above them like they are making jazz hands in the face of oblivion, while everyone else clutches the guard bar. Not me. I choke the throat of the person in front of me and bottle up their scream to make a human air bag.

EMERGENCY BROADCAST SYSTEM

We're blasting the concert on TV, dancing oblivious, when that obnoxious Emergency Broadcast Signal takes over my surround sound equipment. Hella loud. At such volume, we clutch our ears in pain.

A staticky voice reassures: "This has only been a test... If this had been a real emergency... well...."

My speakers explode, killing us all.

DARTS

Not only does he draw a dartboard on my face, but he colors in the numbered wedges with black and red sharpies. He measures the official position, ticks the line on the ground, and throws. I laugh when he misses, but not just because of that. He uses juggling cleavers for darts, so why bother?

DIRTY DIAPERS

I leap from the hospital roof, landing in a steaming dumpster marked *BIOHAZARD*. The bin brims with used diapers; they splash when they catch my fall.

Lacquered in shit, I clamber through a plastic haze of stinky diapers, only to slip and lacerate an artery on a scalpel sticking out of a bloody baby-bearing one.

MER-DUR

My sinking like a stone to the bottom of the sea is experienced in shockwaves. First, I'm shocked that mermaids actually exist! The next shocker occurs when I see their beautiful heads swarm with spark-flashing electric eels. These eels shock me with 650 volts. But it's the Mer-Medusa's gaze that ultimately turns me to stone.

AMUSEMENT PARK RIDE #3: FERRIS WHEEL

I trip as I'm climbing into the Ferris Wheel cart, but nobody notices. My left foot catches between the brushed aluminum floorboards, but nobody sees. I complain that I'm stuck but nobody responds. Each cart bumps me in the head as it passes, but no one pays heed. The carny pushes the accelerator and smiles.

GRAPEFRUIT SPOON

It's such an evil device, this grapefruit spoon. Half-knife, half-scoop, it slides between my lips as easily as a fresh cut Ruby Red. I probe around the scalloped edges with my tongue and slurp it right off the spoon in the process. It's hard to distinguish between pink fruit and red muscle—both taste bitter.

THE RACK

I always wondered if the arms or the legs would give out first if I ever found myself stretched on The Rack.

I'd have bet on the arms.

But it's a draw: one leg pops from my pelvis in sync with my left arm. The torturer stretches me into a disco pose, awaiting the tie-breaker.

A THOUSAND CUTS

Wait, Mr. Executioner! The State specifically sentenced me to *lingchi*. Death by a thousand cuts. That's one thousand. By my count you're at 999. Only *one* remains! You haven't touched my genitals yet, and I thank you for creatively avoiding them, but with these scars I'll never date again, so, balls away! Not—my—throat!

FAST FOOD

"Let me read your order back to you: One Happy Time Meal, with double meat, shredded lettuce, Zika skeeter proboscises, onions, rusty staples, poisoned rat droppings, fried peyote, pickled private parts, extra scab, phlegm, and gun barrel-fried bacon on a demon seed bun dusted with cremated clown ash. Is that correct?"

Almost. Hold the gun.

AMUSEMENT PARK RIDE #4: CAROUSEL

I am strung up to the rafters of the carousel ride. All the shiny king's horses eyeball me with porcelain glares, some raising hooves like they want to ask a question. But I know they're actually rearing to kick me as the carousel starts to spin, taking the stool out from underfoot in the process.

PINOCCHIOTOMY

The EMT says he has to perform an emergency Pinocchiotomy. He pulls out a long pair of iron pincers—medieval-looking, like something out of the Black Forest.

"Hold on! What is that?"

"Bone extractor," he says. "Your skeleton is all wood, right?"

"Of course not!"

He eyeballs my face. "Liar!"

He starts with the nose.

ALIEN PROBE

I writhe naked as they lift my legs with pincers. A telescoping robotic prod moves into position, like some insanely large rectal thermometer. It spits out a squirmy bit—a twitching green stalk with an eye. I hesitate, but let go, shitting in its face—releasing the fusion grenade I've snuck into the alien nest.

PAPERWORK

The boss told me to digitize our insurance company archives. I gave him my middle digit instead. I could burn all that garbage, none the wiser.

I scanned enough to keep up appearances, then struck a match. Flames spread. Heat rose as I cackled. Then the scanner exploded in a fireball of glass and shrapnel.

KNIVES

I confessed I never liked her cooking. So for dinner my wife serves up revenge. It is cold. And metallic.

She uses the fancy silverware to dish it out. Surgical slices and painful pricks.

For her final course: I swallow a dessert made of magnets and she tosses blades over her shoulder, like wedding bouquets.

AMUSEMENT PARK RIDE #5: THE VORTEX

The Vortex spins so fast they drop the floor and everyone is held against the cylindrical wall by centrifugal force and we laugh at each other defying gravity until the machine gun turrets drop in the center of the room, spinning and shooting and the ride doesn't stop until the blood rises to our feet.

MORPHSUIT

It's tight, but I love how unrecognizable I become in my gold morphsuit. The fabric clings to my flesh, but you don't even know what color I am inside. When I remove my costume it sticks and peels my skin right off with it, and though the pain is unbearable, I grin, finally, permanently, unrecognizable.

OFFICE BUILDING

A rumble above, like God's coughing, and we instinctively look up, bearing our necks, opening our mouths, squinting over noses. But when your office building collapses above you, you're lucky if you get to enjoy a moment of sky before you drown in all that falling furniture, that flurry of floorboards, that frenzy of friends.

SEAHORSES

Seahorses are the zombified torsos of retired ancient Roman centurion stallions that were dismembered and given an ocean burial. I know this because a troop of them ganged together and head-butted me into unconsciousness before they chewed off my limbs. Now I am a seahuman. I ride the nightmares, galloping the seven seas for brains.

ARCHERY

I am found five hundred and fifty-five years into the future, skeleton impaled to a petrified tree by a high tech arrow amazingly engineered to take down a mutant grizzly bear in just one shot! But there aren't any bears anymore so no one understands these relics of war: my empty skull, this godforsaken arrow.

AMUSEMENT PARK RIDE #6: THE HAUNTED HOUSE

The Haunted House ride is for babies: a carriage tour of plastic cut-outs—creatures that slowly spring out and weakly scream at you in the dark.

But I'm locked in the cart. It never stops. On the fiftieth tour, I cry for help from the people in line, but they just glare at me, bored.

FATE

My mystic draws the final card of my tarot spread... and gasps.

I expected the Death card, but it's the Hanging Man.

I drop my head in relief.

She reads the cards. "There's a traitor in your life..."

And then the assassin above lets go of his rope and falls, katana swinging toward my neck.

FIRE

Any last words?

"I get 'dust to dust.' Our cells *are* living dust. And dead skin is even floating in the dust. But what's with 'ashes to ashes'? Who's made up of ashes? Not even this cigarette. Sure, there's cremation. But shouldn't we say 'dust to ash'? Or 'creme to creme'? Or..."

Ready... Aim... Fire!

GIANT MUTANT TICKS

Ticks are lazy. They loiter in brush, hopping a ride if they're lucky, and burying their head in their dinner plate. But giant mutant ticks are different. They bloat so big that they eventually grow appendages on their back larger than yours, and after you're drained they carry you to the bus stop and wait.

POLITICAL ANIMALS

I am being trampled to death by elephants chasing—and being chased back by—donkeys.

In this sick circus, an Uncle Sam clown directs me to a red lever.

That lever decides which beast lives.

I crawl amid the tumult. Grab it. Pull...

But voted for neither.

A trap door opens and I am hanged.

AMUSEMENT PARK RIDE #7: TUNNEL OF LOVE

The neon sign above the cavernous ride entrance reads *Tunnel of Love*. Pink light laps the waves around our boat as I hug my lover closer, hoping she'll kiss me inside.

The sign splashes into the water, electrifying the moat.

We sizzle and spasm in shock—and in the air between us, we swap spit.

LEAF PILE

What a tall pile of leaves! I must dive in! The fluffy crackle of it all is exhilarating. There's nothing on Earth like leaves tussling in a feathery plume, browning the air above while I tumble in red flannel and oak. But this red is blood. A steel rake fingers my spine. Help! I've fallen.

SPACKLE

I have drums of spackle in my shop. So when I accidentally shot my hand with a nail gun, I was thankful. I plugged the bloody hole with so much I could feel the grit crunching between my knuckles. But when I later pulled the pink plug, I fainted and painted the floor with blood.

INSOMNIA

I rolled my tired eyes beneath their lids and turned to cliché: counting sheep. One by one, the fuzzy balls of yarn happily hopped a fence. I think I was put to sleep around five hundred and fifty-five, because then, *en masse*, the herd attacked, smothering me beneath a gigantic, writhing pillow of living wool.

BONES

The femur is the most painful bone, of course, but size doesn't matter. Any bone with girth could be used as a club, sure, but even a knuckle could be sharpened to shiv. But it's not about pain. It's about the embarrassment of being boned to death by another man. Especially your wife's paramour's pelvis.

AMUSEMENT PARK RIDE #8: LOG FLUME

It feels like milling around aimlessly in 1950s kitsch at first, but soon the cool and chaotic splashing is pleasant as the flume picks up speed. Channels of water propel our hollow log up a tall slope to the finale: a dead-dropping splashdown before an awaiting logging saw that mists the audience with our blood.

ASPHYXIATION

My murderer shoves a retail bag over my head, tied off with a zip cord. My mouth sucks only plastic—no air. He lets me lumber around the room, struggling for breath, seeking escape. It's a bag from Target. The bullseye logo is over my face; through it I see a shadow aiming a gun.

DRILL

The driller killer *really* means business, wearing his construction cap, goggles, apron, and gloves. He has me secured, spread-eagled atop a large, laminated U.S. map on the floor. He surgically drills his holes and places tiny wooden lattices above each wound. He dances action figures under the spurting red geysers of my blood, crying "Oil!"

DIABETES

The needle disposal bin above the paper towels is brimming with hypos. Disgusting. How many diabetics are in this casino?

A stall bursts open. A haggard man approaches, needles porcupining from both fists.

I direct him to the overstuffed bin.

"Sugar!" he shouts, knocking me down, jabbing them in and sucking out my blood. "Sugar!"

SUET CAKE

I'm in a drugged stupor when my neighbor submerges me in her bathtub brimming with lard. She empties sacks of seed over my chest, weighting me down in the muck. I awaken in her backyard, frozen solid in a block of hardened fat. A starling lands. It considers my eyes the entire time it pecks.

AMUSEMENT PARK RIDE #9: BUMPER CARS

I am climbing out of my cart when I'm gently bumped, and trip out onto the concrete. An oncoming cluster bumps chaotically against one another, dimly reminding me of TV commercials for "scrubbing bubbles"—when one cracks my skull, and another smears my brains under his rubbery carriage like foamy bird shit beneath a squeegee.

CAFFEINE

What the glorious fuck *do you mean* you won't sell me another extra-large caramel mocha triple shot latte? I demand to talk to your manager! What?! *You're* the manager? The only thing you've managed to do is fuck up everything I've ordered all day. *WHAT?!* You think I'm gonna overdose on caffeine? You can't overdo....

AUDIOBOOK

It takes a minute for me to realize those high beams ahead are actually on my side of the interstate—and then I'm sailing through a shower of glass, another, my head finally slamming another man's dashboard. A nearby speaker still plays an audiobook. It's some self-help crap, about attaining a better life through hypnosis.

VIRGIN SACRIFICE

We both have pierced noses and tattoos, but the tribal chieftain is not my friend.

"I'm not a virgin!" I cry from the volcano's rim.

"Dunka-punka!" he shouts.

His gobbledygook sounds almost... British.

"I'm male! Doesn't that matter?"

"DUNKA-PUNKA!"

Tribesmen push me closer to lava. I'm sweating.

Cockney? "Dunk a punker?"

They push me over.

BRAIN TUMOR

My brain had become impregnated with too many fruitful ideas. Time grew them tumorous, nestled together like a bunch of green bananas lining the inside of my skull. When the time was ripe to birth, I pushed and my brains squirted out of my eyes and ears. But somehow, nothing came out of my mouth.

AMUSEMENT PARK RIDE #10: THE TILT-A-WHIRL

"Listen, son. The whole Earth is a Tilt-a-Whirl, swinging all drunk around a wobbly axis while simultaneously looping in orbit around a fireball and the whole universe is nothing but an amusement park run by an insane carny called 'God'... so I do this because I love you," he shouted as he pushed me out.

PACK OF WOLVES

The thing about being murdered by a pack of wolves is realizing that the first wolf's jugular bite really was all it took. After that, it's not "murder" anymore as much as it's embarrassing. Why struggle now? Worse than murder is the massacre of your dignity; you're nothing more than sloppy seconds and lucky leftovers.

CORKSCREW

I wink at my gorgeous lover and show off my corkscrew skills by twisting the bottle, not the screw. She squirms in her seat like she's the bottle and I'm the screw. I blush, slipping, and the bottle's neck cracks off as I twist, screwing into my wrist. Blood decants.

She drinks it later, anyway.

LAUGHTER

I love laughing, but I don't want to die laughing, my chortles echoing in the lonely execution chamber as I cackle at my joke about the guard's expert "baton handling" right when the warden turns the switch and my diaphragm twitches, still laughing the air in and out of my wheezing, boiling brown lung tissue.

SWEAT

I am trapped in a giant tank full of sweat. The gathered perspiration of who knows how many people. I float with just a thin sliver of air between the surface and the lid. I wonder: Where'd all this sweat come from? Then I realize, treading heavily: my own sweat will soon top it off.

AMUSEMENT PARK RIDE #11: BOUNCY HOUSEY

I climb into the Inflatable House of Usher just as some kid cuts our anchor. Wind carries us swiftly over a cliff. We tumble—a knife spinning among us—like bones in a dice cup. The house hisses. Children scream. Lacquered in their blood I slicker around, laughing, living it up all the way down.

ROTTEN BED NUTS

Brian Warfield

THIS MEANS A LOSS A GREAT LOSS

At four in the morning, I hear ringing in my ears. I hang up the phone, "Hello?" I look out the window, but it isn't clear. There is only black paper. Someone had come in and replaced everything with their replicas. I picked up the paper phone. I fell asleep through my paper bed. Goodbye.

THE PLACE WAS SHOWN TO BE VERY LIKE THE LAST TIME

The lamp was still on and burning a kind of scented scent. It filled the air and room with an almost physical presence. It pushed everything else to one side, into the corners. I remember having reached my left hand up, even though I am right-handed, and turning it off. I will do it again.

THERE IS COAGULATION IN COLD

A plume of breath clutters the view. One blade goes sizingly along the ice. If we go round and around, flipping in the idle, we make infinities and dull our senses. There is cocoa waiting in the future. We want to make it to beyond. A cut is a cut on ice or over necks.

LITTLE EYELETS THAT HAVE HAMMER

Close their fists around a weapon or tool. Say weapon first, so mean it. With eyes closed it is harder to aim. Raise the hammer above the bell. The eyes are innocent. We are guilty. They have the hammer and I am being hammered. It is the crack of dawn and the hammer is falling.

THIS MEANS A SOLEMN CHANGE

Makes no difference to me. The door is open, closed, something in the middle. Everything that rises, rises within me. I can feel it on my insides, making a work. Battle scars and galacticuts. Everything becomes another thing like illusions and fantasies. I have my eyes open. I have my eyes closed. The space between.

HE HEAT IT HEAT EATING

He makes me an open-faced sandwich beside still waters. He eats a hot jacket pocket. They that denim shall wait for another generation to cool. In the side pocket is a ham and Swiss Army knife. The microwave is a tiny queen. Inside the queen, cheese comes with holes. He puts his tongue through whole.

A CURVING EXAMPLE MAKES RIGHTEOUS FINGERNAILS

They grow to the left to scratch at open window sills. Still no proof that I am alive. Yawing into my hand, keratin cut. Little cords installed attached to bells the dead to wake. The moon bends around a forked tree to make a wish and scoop out worms lowered into loam, catching the time.

NOTWITHSTANDING AN ELEPHANT

The cannibals gave up meat for Lent. They crossed the Alps to pick turnips that were buried there by the Maori tribe. The roots were shaped like elephants' ears and prepared by dipping into vats of coffee. The cannibals were satisfied for forty days, after which they killed and ate the Romans on graham crackers.

A SINGLE IMAGE IS NOT SPLENDOR

The sun setting over Alhambra. The photograph of it. I hold it in my hands, on one side the signature of my lover. The paper is heavy in my hands. He loves me, the sun says as it kisses down over spires and turrets. He loves me not, the other side of the postcard says.

THE KIND OF SHOW IS MADE
BY SQUEEZING

The kind of puppet that hangs on strings. Children clapping at a beheading. The deepest cut is the kindest. Bright lights, lots of colors flashing. Mnemonic device for seizures. Hey, kids, let's all hold hands. You reach for my hand but it's a bloody stump. What do you do in the absence of a tourniquet?

NO CUP IS BROKEN IN MORE
PLACES AND MENDED

The cracks are where the water runs through. The water fills up a trough, runs down the angle of it. Tips out through a funnel to turn the wheel's axle. The axle spins, tightening the string, lifting the lever. You're standing there waiting for your egg. Your hands are cupped, but your cup is broken.

A SINGLE FRANTIC SULLENNESS

The first mirror which reflected her face showed a young women. I looked through it, somewhat surprised. Not that she wasn't old, but that she wasn't me. Every few years I would look in the mirror and it would show me the unraveled truth. There I was, staring back at me, a young unspoiled woman.

A WHOLE SPOON THAT IS FULL IS NOT SPILLING

I held it steady. There were loud sounds just outside the window. A cloud bursting full of rubble. The earth shook, or just the building, but not my hand as it held the spoon. I could feel the metal in my hand, squeezed between fingers like just more flesh. Her mouth opened to take it.

BLIND GLASS

Coffee is a biting handdrown mudsling I am causing it to cold. In heatless radiator makes a fine table. Upside swingdown black black on brewed sometimes. Sometimes I hope comes in the morning. In the dark, I make blind coffee in black glass made unmade gulping wake. Make a mourning in dark of bloodwine ready.

WHY IS A BONE OUTSTANDING

I've never broken a bone. I've broken a window. When I bend my arms in imitation of flying, the fibula resists. I plummet to the earth. You look at me like *what's your problem.* I lack the proper imagination. You scold me. Tell me to get my act together. I wear a cast for months.

A WET CUP MEANS A VACATION

I need a wetness in my cuppal area. I need full rivers running through them. Exiting doors, vanishing in the mid. I opened the cupboard and they were gone. I needed to wet my whistle. I was in a rented cottage. Complete with costumed characters serving me. If I closed my eyes, I'd wake up.

SHAVED WITH AN OLD MOUNTAIN

There were rivers and trees and swarms of gnats residing inside the medicine cabinet. I went to shave this morning and pulled out a trout. I rubbed the trout along my stubble and we peeled each other's skin off. There were crags. And goats and wispy clouds just on the other side of my reflection.

NOT A RAZOR LESS

The water is running from the mountain through the faucet down the drain to the sea. My hands interfere only minutely. That is, for one minute. I lift my hands to my face with water cupped. There is shaving cream there. Under the shaving cream, my face is only a blank white sheet of paper.

THEY DO NOT EAT WHO MENTION SILVER AND SWEET

Their mouths are full of cavities. Their stomachs are full of babies. Their teeth are razor sharpened. Their feet are hairy and huge. They do not mention what their fillings are cast from or the flavor of the babies. They do not speak of such. Their mouths are full of bones and brittle. They hunger.

A FACT IS THAT WHEN THE PLACE WAS REPLACED

They returned to find it missing. They searched in all of the closets, or tried to. They opened the doors to the closets, where it might have been, to find only smooth wall. They had left a light on but found only darkness. They had gone on vacation, but now it had followed them home.

ANY LITTLE THING IS WATER

She got a penny lodged in her throat trying to drink it. She tried washing it down with a mustard seed. A spider was made out of water. Little things carefully stacked upon other little things build an ocean. The ocean is made out of a mountain of sand pebbles. The earth is the sea.

A CAPE IS A COVER

The canaveral is tied around the neck and over the face. It winds itself parasitically over the face of the face latching on to the orifices with tendrils which snake in and hook. The canaveral leaches its sustenance from the host face. It causes the host to flit about and enact deeds of suicidal heroism.

A SINGLE LINE AND A STAIRWAY

In the dark. Hands outstretched un-stubbedtoeingly. Fetching glasses of something to drink. One million hassocks as barriers. I was blind anyway, could have been any year at all. Could have been clear sailing here to Gibraltar. We lived on a single floor. There shouldn't have been any stairs anywhere. Shouldn't have been an open grave.

IT DOES AND THEN
WHEN IT IS SETTLED

It keeps doing. It does while it is settling and even afterwards. Does it ever not is the question. It does, i.e. it does do not. Not now. Not prior to its settling or in the midst or after. But at some random point when you might least expect. Like the now and prior nots.

A WINDOW HAS ANOTHER SPELLING

Which is French for bread, which is baguette. They ate the whole loaf on their picnic with chateaubriand and camembert. They rode bicycles, and the wheels of their tires turned and turned. They slept upon sandy beaches and got burned by the sun. When they slapped each other, they left white prints on red skin.

THERE IS A DISTURBANCE

Shaking a hand at a morgue. I've got the chocolate shakes. The jitterbug critters. Crawling down my back like a severed morgue hand. A trail of blood, tears, and breadcrumbs leads me back to my home. Home is where the telltale heart is. In a chest locked in the dark forest. In a forgotten cottage.

HARM IS OLD BOAT

Ham is a pig on a sandwich. What's the ham in trying. A sandwich on a boat is a catastrophe. Oars and everything flailing. What's the use in rowing o'er and o'er. Ham sandwich, please, with slices of bread like a life preserver. Mayonnaise on an old boat keeps it from sinking, the dead boar.

THE RESEMBLANCE BETWEEN THE CIRCULAR SIDE PLACE AND NOTHING ELSE

That is to say they were identical. At least at a glance. The circular side place when crossing a crowded room would turn the same (not just the same number of, but the exact same) heads as nothing else. When talking to each other, you'd think it was a mirror and one of them crazy.

IT COULD BE ANY BLACK BORDER

Thick, congealed brink around dead meat. The ooze between two hands shaking. Pull apart and the goo sort of stretches out between. The ectoplasm of living room wallpaper. The downy-haired surface of ear placed against an eavesdrop. The magical marking on my map where I trace where to break in. Your shattered plastic toy chest.

IT DOES NOT MEAN THAT EXUDATION IS CUMBERSOME

Falling down even more steps. A pallet on his back. He gets up and looks over his shoulder. His blood traced his trail. A groove down his back a gulley. He feels it beading up back there, coating the pallet. He needs to make better time. He hunches over experimentally. Something is dislodged and prickling.

THERE IS A WHOLE CHANCE TO BE REASONABLE

I handed you with my hand that chance. An opportunity for a handshake or to lay some skin. Maybe you didn't know what it was or that it was one whole of one instead of just its half. We are poor, it's true, and will slip some on the flip side if you're not careful.

A LITTLE SIGN OF AN ENTRANCE

There are more exits signs than entrance. You are more inclined to get lost in small spaces. There are large, brightly lit signs showing the way out of closets. No one ever gets lost in the outdoor world. Maybe when you do you're gone for good. When you exit the world, there's no coming back.

THE TIME CAME WHEN THERE WAS A BIRTHDAY

I've been waiting for it all my life. The livelong day when I'll be born. I'm holding my breath in the no-zone. Everyone's getting tailored for their birthday suits. I literally cannot wait. I rush and grab a spare rib. It doesn't really fit me. I pull it over my shoulder like an awkward monster.

AN EXAMPLE OF THIS IS FIFTEEN YEARS

An example of a five dollar bill is the Spanish-American War. An example of a pineapple is Missouri. An example of an exam is oncology. An example of an execution is a mirror. An example of a tuxedo is a teddy bear. The Vietnam War lasted sixteen years and is an example of an extraction.

REALLY LILACS ARE DISTURBED

At night you feel it staring through your window. You feel a presence. As you sleep, you feel a weight hanging over you, waiting to suffocate you. You can tell someone or something is following you in the empty parking garage as you go to your car. There are cut lilacs in the driver's seat.

THIS MAKES A CERTAINTY A SHADE

At midnight the sun is sleeping. You crawl under a rock to look for it. There are only worms there. The worms are sleeping. You wake them up by putting them in your mouth. Now there is no sun even though you are still awake. You need to get to that place inside your mouth.

ANY SPACE IS NOT QUIET IT IS SO LIKELY TO BE SHINY

There is no screaming, but a gentle hissing. It is not as likely to be dull if in space. The rockets are gleaming and dark, like with no atmosphere. All senses depend on a medium. Air passing through a small space. Something leaking through a valve. If you have a puncture, you can see it.

DOES GLIDING MEAN MORE

He had his white socks on a polished floor. His gun wasn't topped and his mission was yet possible. The years were golden, hair auburn, eyes still the same chestnut brown. His face was chiseled according to the Golden Ratio with an ice pick no stone had yet trammeled. He was cruising towards the clearing.

A LAPSE OF CUDDLES

Do you miss me. Do you miss my soft parts. Do you want to nuzzle my gizzards. I miss you awfully. It has been how long since I held your arms in my pants. It has been too long since your skull was nestled within my pelvis. Soon we must slide our wet parts together.

COME IN TOWN LIGHT KITE

A clown on stilts says a bird. Down by the river like pants stripes. The rooftops where the crow's clown feet touch down. The beak is a weapon in clown hands in clown car off the forest out of the river where trout spawn. A hand reaches out from the shallows grasping the kite string.

BUILD IS ALL RIGHT

Destroy is okay, too. But better to place one brick on the top of prior brick. One thing after another. Like the fix. The fixture of sculpture. We can gild you. Brick on brink like a floyd wall. It apart until none is left and all is right. Build break again over and over.

WHEN SINCE, A NO SINCE, A NO, A NO SINCE A NO SINCE, A NO SINCE, A NO

We did, you and I. We ate at that restaurant, we caught that bus, we burned down those pueblos. You pointed your finger; I pulled your trigger. We walked into that bank, right into that vault, we stepped in that blood, we drowned in doubloons. You were driving, but it was me at the wheel.

NO BREATHING IS PAINSTAKING

The pain in my ribs is coming from something else. I take a pain from the pain cushion and jab it under the short ribs. I feel some kind of sensation. Life is short and sweet like barbecue sauce. I inhale a needle, feel it pierce all of the fleshes I have buried in there.

CERTAINLY THE TARGET IS CLEANED

Dusting the bull's eye. Getting the tip all polished. The bull is angry. It is huffing through its nose like a cartoon version and turning red like the basketball team mascot. I run around dribbling and wearing large shorts with a rag made out of a torn-off jersey, forcefully taken, and a can of pledge.

TO CONSIDER A LECTURE

The lobster stands at the podium. The lobster is a telephone. When you pick it up you make a speech. Podium is an opium. You open your mouth and place it under your tongue. The opium tastes like shellfish and butter. You look at the crowd listening and imagine them all naked. You are horny.

AND ALSO A FOUNTAIN

There is grey marble in the grey marble. And veins like plants. Is marble a plant. The courtyard made of plants. Made of rocks. Rocks are made out of veins out of blood, beating heart rocks, bleeding. In the middle of the courtyard, bubbling up all this blood, the cold hard rock plant, my blood.

THIS IS A MONSTER AND AWKWARD QUITE AWKWARD

I sit in the closet on a small chair. There are shirts all around me. I just wanted to make you laugh. That girl's arm looked funny, anyway. I was just joking. There is a rabbit here. He's like me; his name is Bjorn. I pluck off all the little hairs to hide my tears.

THE CARE WITH WHICH THERE IS A CHAIR

Chair where you would like. He said there were no tables plus. Said no mixed metaphors. Chair like a back and seat and legs. A prototype of one of those elements. Carbon or something. Like out of your back it might spring. Like wings that you could sit on. Something so natural as breathing chair.

THE DISGRACE IS NOT IN CARELESSNESS

There were probably a million flights of stares I was subjected to. The round eyeballs were tidy in their staring and abject objectification of my person. They were not lazy nor half-assed in their judgment. I felt it quite thoroughly and assumed I must have come up failing. The results were sealed in an envelope.

PLEASE SHADE IT A PLAY

You rattle the bones and toss out the runes. A clatter of sixes shakes down on the missive. You forgot to huff luck on them. You suck your teeth and tongue the pips too late. Your pawn moves down the grid and likewise the ticker of lives. Your next turn edges you over the line.

CLIMB UP IN SIGHT CLIMB

There is a limb and a lime at the heights if you can limp hike. You need a sigh with an eight on the side. At the same time, if you clump the blimp pine, a sump chime will sit tight. Lips might quit in the night clip if big mugs bite the chip plight.

A LITTLE CALM IS SO ORDINARY

Dread pirates pulled over the dinghy off the Pacific Ocean, demanding tax and sex. We were transporting a cargo of tacks and secks. That was where the confusion began. The primates were wearing beards and eye patches and pulled our pants down somewhere in the vicinity of our ankles. Then they pulled out their cutlasses.

SUGAR IS NOT A VEGETABLE

Sugar is meat. I slice it off the creature I find huddling in the basement. The creature comes out at night. It looks mostly like a rat exposed to gamma rays. The creature has terrible fangs and claws and doesn't die when you strike it. You must lull it to sleep to render the sugar.

THE SAME FURNITURE

Fuck it, let's just move the couch, bureau, bookshelf into the middle of the room, let's just keep pushing until the window gets bigger, eats it all, let's make the bed bigger, let's ditch the hutch, say goodbye to the chabudai, hasta la vista to the accubita, we'll live out of suitcases, ready to split.

CHANGING AND EXTERNAL AND CENTRAL AND SURROUNDED AND SINGULAR AND

From the bang's big pulse outward organisms orgasm bigger om's like a closed-eyed monk funking ohms it hertz good goo to hay I oh everything natural sequence desire multitudes forcing down facing dog gold spinning records play act minus one almost here it is here coming down to appoint resolve revolution circle pinpoint prick birth.

COPYRIGHT PENDING

John Edward Lawson

HEALTHY

I use a razor to peel away the skin of my inner right arm to determine if you can still suffer.

You have no reaction.

I use that razor to peel away the skin of your inner right forearm.

I feel nothing.

Pressing our wounds together permits our diseases to co-mingle.

We're a perfect match.

FOURTH WALL WRECKING BALL

The victims from every horror movie came back.

The victims from every ninja movie returned.

The victims from every uncensored hentai came back.

The victims from every romance movie reappeared.

To the real world, to our streets and homes, not the silver screen or boob tube.

And they were seriously pissed.

Roll closing credits, motherfucker.

INVETERATE DICKLESSNESS

An author sits down to compose something scathingly metafictional about the state of the publishing industry, of authors, of readers, of what passes as an educational system in contemporary society, but is too fragile to face the fact he doesn't have the intellectual tools for the task, and instead eats another seventeen cans of Pringles.

EINSTEIN CAN SUCK IT

My childhood self met my adult self, dropkicking my future self in the most sensitive of my reproductive parts, shouting, "How you turn out like dis, beeeeeeeeeeeeeeech?!"

My adult self went crying around to anybody who would listen that how things turned out was all my childhood self's fault.

My future ghost pulled the trigger.

DEAREST WISH

I went back in time to view my mother once more, as she was in her youth.

She was wearing hot pants that must have been designed by gynecologists, twerking while hitting a hookah, ranting about being a bad bitch.

On returning to the future I invested my fortune in family planning and munitions manufacturing.

HEMATOPOIESIS

Amelia Gulbranson

MAT THE CAT

Once upon a time there was a cat named Mat. Mat the Cat was very naughty. One day it was Thanksgiving. Mat the Cat hated holidays, so he went under the table. Suddenly he jumped up. He bumped the table and the turkey went flying! Then he said the f-word and everybody was really mad.

THREE TYPES OF HAUNTED

The scene is an abandoned hospital in England. Nobody goes there except one person. That person is Morrissey. There had been an apocalypse—only he had survived it. Dead bodies lay all over the ground. Morrissey had rabies. He lived in the abandoned hospital, in a blanket fort, talking to ghosts from around the world.

BABY DERBY

There's a group of little babies who love to roller skate. They were all friends but were sometimes mad at each other. That's when they decided to do roller derby! Their teams were called Rhinoceros Pink, Solar Coke, Satan's Claw, Roller Butt, and Satan's Other Claw. They kicked butt and were best in the league.

GRENDEL

Once, a black crow named Beocrow pecked a monster's arm off. But he was still alive, and his name was... Grendel. The crow came back to his home and said "I got an arm!" The crow didn't like his wings. He cut off one of his wings and attached the monster arm. Grendel was mad.

MURDER DOLL

Candice was the cutest doll. One night on a full moon, another doll named Frances bit her hand. The bite was so painful. On another night with a full moon, a little girl went to play with her Candice, but it wasn't Candice. And something wasn't just quite right. Now *Frances* was the cutest doll.

THE MAGIC HOUSE

The magic house had twenty-four inhabitants, but between them they only had one eye. The magic house had one girl with twenty-four eyes. The magic house was crowned with an enormous Barbie doll head. The magic house had a kitchen where chefs cooked glass butts for dinner. The magic house had a teensy mouse. *SQUEAK!*

REPAIRMAN ASSASSIN

Someone's limousine was broken. They called the limousine repairman. When he showed up, he stared at them strangely. He started to bounce on top of the car like a trampoline. In a deep voice that sounded like an assassin, he said, "Come join me." They refused. In the distance you could hear sounds of choking.

BOBBY'S LUNCH

Once there was a flying pig. He asked a passing human if they could fly. "No, I cannot fly. We are not flying pigs." The pig came to an inchworm.

"Can you fly?"

"No, I cannot. We are not flying pigs." The flying pig flew up to a fox named Bobby.

"Can you fly, Bobby?"

GROWLERS

Growlers was a type of beer—a very fancy beer. The taste was so sour, you would spit it out onto your family. Bob's family got really mad when he did that to them. The smell was so bad that everyone thought he was drinking toilet water. His Growlers farts made everyone run away screaming.

LEAF MAN
(a song)

Leaf man leaf mean leaf man,
    leaf man leaf man leaf man
Leaf man sang songs about himself
Leaf man sleeps up on a shelf
He used a leaf for toilet paper
Leaf man was crazy
He ate caterpillars for his dinner
Leaf man never ate people food
Leaf man leaf man leaf man
Pow!

BLOODY DEATH ON THE HIGH SEAS

Once there was a pirate who had no ship. She didn't need a ship. She was a mermaid. She would swim out to ships and sink them. Then her crew of sharks would eat the survivors. She was the best captain ever, because she gave her crew what they wanted most: fish sticks and blood.

ZEBRA KITE

A little girl had a favorite kite that was painted with a picture of a zebra. One night it came to life. A few days passed and the little girl's friends began to go missing. She was very scared. Holding a stuffed animal in her room, she heard a noise at the door. *Zebra hooves.*

GHOSTLY

They are bad. No, seriously, they are really really bad. What? They are sad, because of their cause... of death. What? It's not my fault they're dead. Mean and cruel? They should go to Hell! Bloody Mary killed them. They can't eat anything. They're ghosts; it will fall right through them. They suck. So much.

COFFEE MACHINE

Once there was an evil scientist. One day his invention went wrong. He had tried to make a robot, but he accidentally made a robot spider. Even though it was his invention, he was scared. The spider robot interfaced with the coffee machine and drank everyone's coffee and began multiplying itself, taking over the world.

THE SHAPE

The shape of your buns, the shape of your buns
Not the shape of your face
Shape of your buns, the shape of your buns
Actually, it is the shape of your face
But it's not the shape of your feet
It smells like your feet, though
Your face
Has the shape of your buns

ANCIENT SALT (AND PEPPER)

Once there was a war. There weren't any people—it was salt against pepper. Pepper thought that he was better, as he could make all the children sneeze. Salt thought that he was better because he didn't. They fought with swords and spears. It went on for a while, and never stopped until the end.

CUP DRAGON

A long time ago, a little dragon lived with his mother in a giant-sized teacup. His mother cooked all his favorites—pickle-chiffon pie, snail shell salad, and grilled villager. His mother also let him drink Coke. His mother drank champagne with her snail shell salad. The little dragon was happy; his mother was happy, too.

NINJA BIKO

The sword clashed against the enemy's sword as Biko the Mouse jumped off the roof. His enemy was a ninja cat. The Grand Master Peacock was hidden in a cloth that looked like his feathers. Suddenly, a smoke bomb went off. Ninja Bear stepped from the shadows. Biko shouted at them, "Hey, you dumb ninjas!"

DADDY, THE CLUMSY MAN

Daddy, the Clumsy Man, was walking in the forest. Suddenly a bear attacked him. He was running and running. Some villagers nearby heard him screaming and yelling. They took him back to their house. He tripped and fell over everything—their bread, their milk, and their eggs. Finally, they put salt and pepper *on him*.

THE BLACK FAN

There was a lady in China named Montain. She was eighteen and lived on her own. Her village was destroyed in a war. The Huns burnt down her house with her family in it. Montain had no friends. She had lived in that house since she was twelve. She barely spoke, but lived in peace.

CAR CATASTROPHE

One day every car came crashing into every other car. One person was trying to get to the store, one person was trying to get to a port-a-potty, another was trying to get to a restaurant. All of the cars tried to stop bumping into each other, until someone yelled, "Stop..." then started yelling, "FIRE!"

OWLHOOD

Owlhood was a very bad owl. He wasn't friends with any of the other owls. He was very mean to them. On a blustery day Owlhood flew into a big tree. It belonged to a rich owl. The rich owl did not like him to be in the house, stealing dead mice for the poor.

RED FLAMINGOS

One day a group of flamingos got into nuclear waste, and grew bigger and bigger, until they started to eat people. That's why they were called *red* flamingos. Red... *with blood.* People got really mad but the flamingos started kicking their butts up and down. You never know what flamingos will do to you.

"AAAAAIIIIIEEEEE!"

UNICORN ZOMBIE APOCALYPSE
With apologies to Borgore and Sikdope

Boom! Suddenly someone came running out of their house, yelling, "UNICORN ZOMBIE APOCALYPSE!" Then five, ten, fifteen... sixty unicorn zombies came from the house, too. A bunch of people saw them and started running everywhere, grabbing torches and pitchforks to kill the zombies. Little boys even grabbed their BB guns. There was no turning back.

AYE AYE, CAPTAIN CUTTLEFISH

"Aye aye, Captain Cuttlefish! How ya be today?"

"I be fine today, lad. How about you go swab the decks!"

"Aye aye, Captain Cuttlefish!" He went to swab the deck, but suddenly a giant sea monster rose! It was trying to sink the ship. Along came Mama Cuttlefish—and she was mad.

"STOOOOOOP," she yelled!

TINY WALL

There once was a mouse named Musselbaum. That was his name because he had a lot of muscles. The wall of his house was so tiny even he could step right over it. It kept out ants, because they already had lots of sugar. Musselbaum wanted to impress the princess in the castle next door.

BREAD BURROW

A little piece of bread ran away from a baker. He lived in a little burrow that he had dug. He had eighty-five brothers and sisters from his loaf. He had no parents. You don't want to ask me why. He was very happy with his brothers and sisters. He loved them most of all.

TREE OF FRIENDS

Alice had a very very big treehouse. It was the treehouse of her friends. She had a lot of friends but was also very rich. She didn't care about being rich and wanted to give her money to others. One day she took $200 and gave it to a school. Her parents grounded her forever.

BOUNCY HOUSE FACTORY

This is the factory. The factory for bouncy houses. But here is the weird thing about it... the bouncy houses are alive! An evil scientist brings them to life to create an unstoppable army. One of the bouncy mattresses breaks and he says "I'll get this fixed for someone to sleep on." His army grows.

THE SOLAR PROWLER

The Solar Prowler steals power from the power lines. He is like a ninja, but *reversed*. He can't sneak anywhere because his clothing glows like the sun. The Night-time Beast is his mortal enemy, and tries to shut him down because he messes up the darkness and light. These warriors have battled like this forever.

FLAT-BOTTOMED GIRLS

One day a group of girls went to work. Their friends all had big *butts*. One of the girls' pants fell down. That happened to the other girls, too. They had flat butts. Everybody laughed and laughed. They all started to cry. There was nothing they could do about it. It was a great ending.

UPTOWN COFFEE

Look, this is my bone right here. All that skin on it. The blood. All of that could be off right now, leaving just the bone. No more protective layer. Ah, I see. I've been drinking too much coffee. He's being rude. The cappuccino maker is being rude. You: you're being a jerk right now.

LASER UNICORN CAT

Laser Unicorn Cat came stomping into New York City! Lasers shot from his eyes, hitting the tallest skyscraper there. It was 700 feet tall. Pretty tall, but not anymore. Suddenly the giant beast turned into a cute little kitten wearing a unicorn hat. A marine started shooting at it, and that just made it mad.

AUNTIE, COME OUT OF THE CLOSET

"Auntie, get out of the closet!" God, what is taking her so long. "Can't you hurry and pick out your clothes already?" Why is she taking so long? "Auntie... are you pooping in the closet?"

"Nooooo..."

"Okay, I'm coming in. Jesus, Auntie, did you have diarrhea?"

I look down at the pile of poop.

COLORS

What is your favorite color? Yellow.
What is your favorite color? Purple.
What do yellow and purple make when they're mixed? Brown.
I wasn't asking you. I was asking her.
What do yellow and purple make when they're mixed? Brown.
Okay, now I'm going to ask you a question.
Why are you being a jerk?

WATERMELON

Once there was an ant. He wanted some watermelon, so he went to a picnic. They had corn, strawberries, lollipops, cheeses... and they had watermelon! He was so happy, he could cry. Of course, he had some of the other foods.

He was full, but he made room for watermelon. It was the best day.

THE NEW ONE

When my mom got pregnant, I was grateful.

"You're having a sister," my dad said.
"Really?"
I was having a baby sister.
At the hospital, my mom was in pain.
"One, two, three, push!"
"OWWW!"
Then my dad told me to come in. There was my new baby sister, lying right on my mom.
"Mommy..."

TRAINWRECK

"Oh... no, no, no, piggy! Ah, there goes my pig!"

Pigs are great animals. They live in a pig pen. They eat from a trough.

"Oh my god, the cow is breaking a board. Why did I leave a loose board there!"

Cows eat grass, wheat, corn, hay, barley, and beet pulp.

Farms are trainwrecks.

THE PIRATE BUTTERFLY

This story is true.

Once upon a time there was a pirate ship. It belonged to Captain Spice, the infamous pirate butterfly from the isle of Tortuga.

He'd been searching the Main for treasure. That night there was a storm. There were big waves. The boat was rocking.

Captain Spice was invaded by a cat!

PEACHES' WORLD

Peaches looks up at a cupcake on a regulation diving board. "It's... so... far!"

This is Peaches' world.

"STOP!"

"Hellooooo..."

"Good bye."

They are very crazy. "CUPCAKE!"

I know this sounds nuts... but it's real. "THPPPPT." They fight a lot.

"Hey... you're dumb."

"...You're dumber!"

They are quite cute.

"I love you!"

That's Peaches' world...

ANYTHING

No, I don't want you to turn that off. Sometimes I get a good feeling. I don't care. I'm bored. I might take a little nap on top of the couch, like a cat. What? *What?*

Okay. I get a good feeling. I can't believe we have that movie. Why am I doing this stuff?

BUDDHA BUSTER

The Buddha was in a dancing competition. It was about to be his turn. He was very nervous. Then someone yelled out "Bust a move!" He went out to the dance floor and somebody yelled "Boooo!" He began to dance to "Whistle" by Flo-Rida. It was the most amazing dance jam ever.

"YOU GOT SERVED."

DARK MARSHMALLOWS

This place is terrorized by the Dark Marshmallows. Evil marshmallows. They coat themselves in dark chocolate sauce so they can hide in the shadows. I even heard one time that they murdered a three year old. Or was that Barney the Purple Dinosaur. I heard he robbed a bank five weeks ago. Damn those marshmallows.

PLUM'S ST. PATRICK'S DAY

'Twas the night before St. Patty's Day. Plum was getting ready. She had made a leprechaun trap! Plum went to bed and waited.

Suddenly, a noise woke Plum up. She had caught a sneaky leprechaun. It was trapped in a pot full of many different ingredients.

But she wasn't going to eat the leprechaun... yet.

MIMOSA CAT

At brunch there was a kitten making a very, very large mimosa. He was making the very large mimosa for his friend, Dave. It was his 70th birthday. Dave was the kitten's owner. Dave was the best owner ever—and he was glad to have a kitten like little Maya. They sipped their mimosas quietly.

CIRCUIT RAPPER

This is the story of MC McCrapper, crappiest robot rapper. His first song was "Crappy Shit." People didn't dislike it—they hated it. Dumb robots liked it—the dumbest. While MC McCrapper was on tour with rap-rockers Very Stupid Robots, the drummer pushed him to the ground. He broke his lip and, luckily, couldn't sing.

UNDERWEAR

"Hey, look under there."

"Under where?"

"Ha, you said 'underwear.'"

"Well, that part wasn't very nice. I never fall for that trick."

"You just did. Hey... look under there."

"Under... what?"

"You're supposed to say 'under where.'"

"Ha. Now *you* said it. That's payback for telling me to say that."

"I'll never do it again."

BLOODY DOUBLOONS OF THE NORTH

It was a stormy night when the *Red Jessica* came rolling in from the north. Another ship, the *Starfish's Ass*, pulled alongside and fired grappling hooks to board the *Red Jessica*. The captain of the *Jessica* was very mad at the *Starfish's Ass*. She would have her own revenge. Then she yelled "*My* bloody doubloons!"

DARK FARTER

There was a guy named Bob. Everyone called him "The Dark Farter." They called him that for a good reason—he farted all the time, and his farts sounded like Darth Vader breathing. How did they smell? Very bad. Five 'verys' bad. Everybody was very mad because he stunk up the house. Silent but deadly.

ROBOT DANCE

Have you ever done the Robot Dance? I haven't, but I've been trying to do it. You basically move like a robot. First, you replace your arms and legs with mechanical arms and legs. Then you add a computer head. But you get to design your own head. Then put an engine in your chest.

ABSOLUTE POKER FACE

You know how Lady Gaga can keep her poker face? I don't believe everyone can keep their poker face. Listen, Lady Gaga isn't just playing a game in her song for a boy. She's not even keeping a poker face. That's how she always looks. The superhero Absolute Poker Face can keep *her* poker face.

LOW

Outside of town is a long, lonely road. I went into the old haunted house at the end of it. The door creaked as I opened it just a smidge. Nobody lived there, but there was a rocking chair still rocking. I went in and saw a very steep staircase. I went down the stairs...

KING PUKE

Of all supervillains in the world, King Puke was the worst. He tried to rob a makeup store in the mall, but ended up in custody. When he escaped, he tried to rob a rich person's house but he ended up cleaning their toilet instead. For his ultimate plan, he tried to sell his puke.

PENGUIN COIL POT

A couple of days ago, maybe a week ago, I made a coil pot for my dad. Before that, I made a little penguin. I made both of those out of clay. I took a little bit of white clay, put it on the botttom of the penguin and stuck him onto the pot. Voila!

BISCUIT MAN

Once there was a handful of wheat that didn't know what it wanted to be. First it was crushed into flour. "AAAAAIIIIIEEEEE!" Then it was baked in a scorching oven. "NOOOOOO!" Finally it had become a biscuit, and it was happy. Until... someone ate him.

"Don't bite the back part of me—*that's my buns.*"

APOPTOSIS

Jonathan Moon

FUCKING A PORCUPINE

Fucking a porcupine is a truly daunting task. It requires steely reserves of nerves and a near-savage commitment to catching your nut. You must remain constantly mindful of those hellishly sharp quills, and should know they possess piercing claws as well. The glory of the bestial copulation leads your daring soul to violent sexual legend.

WHEN THE TREES GOT UP
AND DANCED

The autumn breeze carried with it a haunting melody, and the trees got up and danced. Concrete cracked and rended under their mighty mirth, while great feats of architecture quivered with jealousy. Branches undulating at the sky, trunks thrusting seductively, until roots shriveled, died. It's been hard breathing since, but it was lovely that day.

FIREBUG

I found a firebug cradled in a cattle skull. I offered it my palms to rest in. It skittered into my hands, leaving little third degree tracks and dragging broken wings. I called it Frosty, for irony, and it laughed so hard its tears melted my hands away. Frightened, it returned to the cattle skull.

THE FAMILY MAN GETS REVENGE

The Family Man worked very hard to support his family. To unwind, he went to the horse track.

He ended up owing the Wrong Men money. The Wrong Men didn't think the Family Man could pay them, so they killed his family. Even the baby.

The Family Man killed the Wrong Men one by one.

FRIENDS WITH AN ARSONIST

Luke is always setting things on fire. It gets annoying at parties, like the guy who is always tipping over the ash tray, but far more lethal. Luke burns down houses and churches and funeral parlors. Luke traps people inside beforehand.

Reflected flames shimmer in his eyes.

"We are all on fire anyway," he says.

LARRY OF THE GODDAMNED DESERT

Larry joined the military to kill some goddamned terrorist bastards. He didn't do any top secret black ops, but he did kill a lot of little boys with AK47s. He didn't liberate any villages, but he found he liked raping the women. He'd make them leave their hijabs on so they wouldn't haunt his dreams.

FINAL TRANSMISSION OF RESEARCH VESSEL AT-2313 XRW

Control... I repeat, Control... we are losing it... madness is gripping us now... pressure... dents in the spacecraft... worms eating metal... panic... will lead to mutiny... mark my words... this will end in blood... it always does... losing it... Control... do you copy... we are all dying... it doesn't hurt... but... we... miss... mother... mother...

THE SWAMP WITCH

The Swamp Witch has been stealing children again. The village people keep close count nowadays; exactly six have gone missing in the past two moons. No torch-lit mobs searching, for they all know the Swamp Witch has already plucked out their tiny bones and gobbled them up.

Or so they say to comfort each other.

SENIOR YEAR

Jezzy got knocked up at the family reunion. Cousin Ray took her virginity, and Aunt Pamela gave her bellyache tea.

Jezzy got knocked up at a punk rock show. She traded a blowjob for coat hanger surgery.

Jezzy got knocked up by a married man. He paid for a backroom procedure and never called again.

KENNY THE CLOWN

Most days, Kenny sits around in sweat pants; he has three pairs—green, black, and brown. He smokes cigarettes and plots out kidnappings and rapes. Sometimes, Kenny paints his face and wears his clown suit; three colors—green, black, and brown. He smokes cigarettes and masturbates nervously, but forgets his plans. For now. For. Now.

SALLY THE ROBOT

Sally didn't enjoy being born a human. She'd rather be a robot. Her skin had blemishes and rashes and pimples and such. No robot suffered acne. Her emotions were often manic, but often broke down low. Robots were cold emotionless machines ruled by instruction and reason. Sally wrapped herself in scrap metal, and was content.

OBLIGATORY ZOMBIE STORY

Most of the world died and came back as ravenous flesh-eating zombies. Most of those who survived the worldwide carnage turned out to be murderous sociopathic assholes. Sucked to be alone, sucked to be with others, sucked to be eaten alive by dead people. But that's how it fucking goes in a goddamned zombie apocalypse.

FUNERAL RAIN

The day is gray.

Funeral rain pitter-patters mahogany casket, louder than whimpering priest or sobbing widow.

A cluster of people in black crowded around open grave, shielded by black umbrellas.

More rain, more funerals, to come.

One man, also in black but no umbrella, stands alone away from the crowd.

A gun in his hand.

THE STENCH OF PISS

Reggie don't have no money, no job to earn some. He gets twitches and hears voices. Reggie don't have no house to call home, no bed, no ceiling. His life in a backpack, an alleyway, a park bench. No hugs, no love, no blanket, the warmest thing in his life is the stench of piss.

NEW FRIEND REQUESTS

Anti-Social Anne wraps herself in barbed wire, and screams at strangers on the street. Most run away, doing their all to avoid close contact with the abrasive woman. She follows them, berating them and their children, parents. Some cry, some fight. BJ films and uploads. Yesterday she got 74 likes and three new friend requests.

DREAM MACHINE

I had a dream I invented a machine that converted live humans into energy. All other energy companies died, unable to compete against my endless power source. I fed everyone to the machine eventually. It was fun to watch. So bright at the end—and lonely. I woke up picking scraps of flesh from my teeth.

CAMPING

Went to the mountains, dwelled amongst trees. I lost myself to the glow of embers and the creek's cold culling song. Time's crushing loops spasm in the deep of the forest on moonless nights, becoming meaningless and feeble. Rust on the hatchet stains the bone, one of these days I'll make this place my home.

9-TON HAMMER

Grand DuKar is a long forgotten god once worshipped by pale cannibals. Time ravaged the savages, left the god with none to worship him. The great god slouched to the ground and eventually became a mountain. One day, when humans resume eating each other, Grand DuKar will rise again, smashing all with his nine-ton hammer.

THE BABY THIEF

Emily makes good money stealing babies, selling them to buyers on the black market. She used to be a maternity ward nurse, but the money in baby stealing is just so much better she decided to pursue it fulltime. She quit without giving two weeks' notice, because you just can't trust a baby thief.

WITCHES IN THE WOODS

They gather in the circle of Russian olive trees, cavorting in their sullen bruised nakedness. They chant their obscenities, and carve archaic symbols into their own flesh. They throw ashes into the wind and cackle at the starving birds trying to eat it up. I can't sleep through the witch noises, so I watch them.

ANTICHRISTS

A hateful breeze is blowing up from the valleys of our past, and it will waken the antichrists from their slumber in plain sight. Black smoke blasphemy smells like Rome burning, like Jews in an oven, like flaming crosses. Crusades and inquisitions, propaganda prayers, televised holy wars with atrocity highlight reels. Unholy eyes open, unimpressed.

BARBARIANS AT THE GATES

The barbarians at the gate are unafraid of the massive cauldrons of boiling oil. Brave warriors doused with liquid fire, melting at the walls. The terrible scars are worth the glory.

The barbarians at the gate are unaware of the infestation of rats within. Brave warriors devoured by vermin. Some kingdoms are not worth conquering.

BETROTHED

The lords and ladies of Shadowvale gathered to celebrate the wedding of Lord Aeon of the House Darkwater to Lady Eryka of House Drowning. The gathered company elite, the menu extravagant, Lord Aeon handsome, and the decorations lavish, but Lady Eryka wouldn't have it. She gutted herself upon the wedding altar, having long opposed betrothal.

TOUGH GUY TATTOOS

Lemmy went out and got *LOVE* tattooed across his left knuckles, *HATE* across the right. Hurt like a motherfucker, but made him look tough as hell. He liked to scowl up his face and thrust them in strangers' faces in public places like taverns and libraries. He still got his ass kicked an awful lot.

WRAPPED IN BARBED WIRE

In Kirk's neighborhood, they do backyard wrestling. Kids would jump off ladders and roofs, smashing their opponents through plywood and card tables. Even though he is in his early 40s he still likes to participate. He wraps himself in barbed wire and breaks fluorescent bulbs over their pimply teenage foreheads. Kirk is the heavyweight champ.

DANI DEPRESSING

Dani doesn't try to be miserable, it just happens. She meditates, and tries to begin each morning with meaningful positive affirmations.

She smiles, and tries.

Something always reminds: reality is a hammer set to smash her joys to gray little shards.

And she can't just shrug the sadness away. She turns her hammer on others.

TRADITION

Mathis worships old gods, forgotten by the rest of the world. He reads dusty ancient tomes. He scribbles his studies with virgin's blood. He steals children, and opens them up in sacrifice to his horrible gods.

Their gore stains the altar; he drinks mysterious elixirs from their tiny skulls.

All in the name of tradition.

TRAPPED IN A SLASHER FLICK

"I feel like we're trapped in a slasher flick," Monica said.

Everyone else in the basement of the abandoned mental hospital laughed.

Then the killer struck. He dismembered Todd, disemboweled Charlie, tossed Sally from the third floor. Monica ran, the killer chased her. She screamed, the killer laughed. He caught her, then skinned her alive.

THE BRAWL

The quiet of mid-day is shattered along with the window of Dale's Tavern as Bubba and Bart come crashing out and land in the street.

A crowd gathers silently.

Fists, knees, elbows, grunts as the men try to kill each other.

Bubba slips.

Bart climbs atop, smashes Bubba's skull into pavement.

Bart wins another brawl.

BOOBY TRAPPING THE STAIRCASE

The morning after her stepfather *touched* her, Marlene decided to booby trap the staircase to keep him away. Before bed she dotted the steps with marbles, two pairs of roller skates, and used her purple jump rope as a trip wire.

Expertly, he avoided it all.

So she shoved him as he reached the top.

SUICIDE IN THE SWAMP

Kyle got sick of livin' and decided to end it all.

Told his kin farewell, and walked into the swamp.

Deep in the swamp, alone with the leeches and chiggers and toads, Kyle pulled out his skinnin' knife. Cut his arms, wrists to elbows. Mosquitos buzzed to his wounds. Smiling, he sunk beneath the mire.

363 DAYS WITHOUT AN ACCIDENT

Safety was important at Starshine, Inc. The safety coordinator, Tobias, was very proud of their record. Then, he caught Martin from accounts fucking his wife. He lured Martin into a supply room and tipped shelving holding spare printers onto him.

Tobias' replacement, Bob, wept as he erased "363" and wrote a big sloppy "0" instead.

THE HIT MAN EARNS HIS PAY

In the middle of the busy courtyard, four large men in suits surround a smaller man shouting into his phone.

"Don't you know who I am?!"

A man in sunglasses watches over his newspaper.

"I am Salvatore Vititazzio!"

The man in sunglasses raises gun, lowers newspaper.

Five shots, five bodies.

He disappears into the crowd.

THE WEE SAVAGES OF
BITTER RAW BAY

In Bitter Raw Bay lives a tribe of wee savages. Wee worshippers of meat. Full-on cannibals with skulls on sticks, earlobe necklaces, warm carcass breath, and sharpened teeth. They keep their victims alive for days, skinning them slowly, chopping them apart limb by juicy limb, and forcing them to watch their violent primitive mating rituals.

IN THE GARDEN

When one of Old Lady Hayes' many cats would die of age or distemper or drowning, she would bury it in the garden so the roses would grow. The cats would watch her bury them, one by one. When the cats buried Old Lady Hayes in the garden, the roses could never grow more beautiful.

THE OPIUM DEN

Men shadowed by darkness and smoke are sprawled throughout the room. Simple music, like fingers plucking two copper strings, echoes off the walls and swirls with each exhaled burst of fresh smoke.

A dragon slithers into the room. It eats Wu in front of them. None believe what they see until it is eating them.

SON OF A CARNIE

Milton was born on the midway, birthed in the dust like a real son of a carnie. He was raised up by tent men, barkers, jugglers, and whores. He worked hard and swindled well, raping the ever-changing locals in his spare time. He died on the midway, like his Pa before. As shall his sons.

THE CHASE

All his life, Jason felt like something was chasing him. A pressing dread, a harrowing truth, an uncomfortable sense of inevitability clomping after his every step. A demon unseen but gaining ground.

On the day it caught up, Jason had a stunning moment of clarity—he knew what everything meant. It was over too fast.

LOST IN THE NEVADA DESERT

When Jesse was eighteen, he ate a bunch of psychedelic mushrooms and got lost in the Nevada desert. He found lizards with obnoxious clown-like coloration lounging about performing elaborate mating rituals. While studying them, he was sexually assaulted by a group of men dressed as Tusken Raiders. Jesse doesn't go to the desert any more.

JONAH'S SHEARS

Jonah was an avid wanderer, wandering near and far. He carried shears, shears with smooth wooden handles and long, sharp blades. Jonah wandered with his shears, cutting pieces of himself off and leaving the chopped bits everywhere he visited. He left a thumb in Denver, an ear in Memphis, his left foot in Wichita Falls.

GYPSY ABORTION

Jezzy got knocked up and couldn't afford surgery. She heard of an old gypsy woman forced to live at the edge of town with some Old Country remedies for things like that. Jezzy traded a blowjob for a ride out to the old gypsy's shack. Thirteen bucks for a tea, made her bleed and bleed.

THE HORROR OF VAGUENESS

A thing, a creature, a monster, great and indescribable, arose from eons of restless sleep. It did things, terrible, heinous, and mean, which decent people would not discuss in detail. It drove the world to the brink of madness, though most of them had no idea why. A seething plague, a noxious disease of nothingness.

KILL, KILL, KILL

Jedidiah heard voices. They told him to *KILL, KILL, KILL.*

Jedidiah asked the voices if they were God. The voices said *KILL, KILL, KILL.*

Jedidiah heard voices his family couldn't hear. His family couldn't know the voices wanted him to *KILL, KILL, KILL.*

Jedidiah slaughtered them all, wrote in blood on walls *KILL, KILL, KILL.*

SIX PACK AND
A CIRCLE OF FLAMING HOBOS

Luke and I were cutting through the train yard on our way to Quickie Mart. I just wanted a beer, something to buzz me up, but Luke got distracted when we found the circle of hobos. Luke bought a gallon of gas, six beers. We waited until they passed out, then Luke set them aflame.

CATCHING FLIES

The incessant buzzing of houseflies was seriously dampening the typical calming effects of Tonia's Thursday macramé. Each of her fingers—a different colored string tied to it, together woven into a dazzling potholder, so she chewed on her tongue. Chewed it pulpy, long, and bloody, used it to catch flies with bloody thwacks and gulps.

STARSHINE

Massive waves of irradiated energy swept over the distant space colony with each convulsion of their dying star. All the trees died, babies born mutated, the oceans turned to acid, and politicians debated scientists over the cause. The starshine was twitching, the seasons cannibalizing, but there was money to be made until the starshine faded.

COMMUTING

Nadine rode the 613 bus to and from work. She'd read her tabloids and scribble in her crossword puzzles. No one ever bothered her, each passenger on the bus content commuting unto themselves. Nadine died on the 613 bus of a massive aneurism. Her eyes filled with blood, ran down her cheeks. Commuting unto herself.

WHITTLEBACK ROAD

Way out on Whittleback Road every house is a meth lab just waiting to explode.

Way out on Whittleback Road they hang gypsies from crooked trees and roast stolen goats over bonfires.

Way out on Whittleback Road they worship old gods, dark flesh-hungry deities.

I ain't been to Whittleback Road, but so I've been told.

THE MINOTAUR

Many horrors haunt the halls and corridors of the maze, and many heroes have met their screaming ends there. And of these hall-haunting horrors, among these creators of corpses, none is more vicious than the dreaded Minotaur. It snorts, inhaling the stench of man meat, and savagely hunts down its prey, a furious goring monster.

THE GUN FIGHT

Floyd and Chester disagree. Beer is spilt, chairs overturned, and family names insulted. Only fighting to the death can restore such tarnished honor.

A crowd gathers.

Floyd and Chester take fifteen paces, face each other with hands hovering above holsters.

They draw, fire. Shots ring out, smoke clears.

Chester as dead as his family's honor.

COPS AND ROBBERS

The boys on my block are playing cops and robbers. I have to be a robber, everyone else wants to be a cop. Me and scattered younger brothers as my criminal crew. The cops chase us down one by one. The cops employ questionable interrogation tactics. With my daddy's gun, they're not taking me alive.

TRAILER PARK EXORCISM

Little Travis got into his dad's methamphetamine and ran roughshod through the trailer park. He twitched around in little circles and spoke gibberish. His parents tied him to the bed and called the priest. The priest read from the Bible while Travis convulsed and died. They chalked it up as one more soul for Satan.

COUNTING THINGS IN OLD MAN HANDON'S YARD

One, just one, broken down Chevy up on bricks, eaten by rust.

One, two starving dogs with snarling mouths, ribs showing.

One, two, three black birds cursing down from the trees.

One, two, three, four weeping willows shading crooked shack, dying grass.

One, two, three, four, five shallow grave stone piles with rickety wooden crosses.

CONSUMED BY THE UNRELENTING URGE TO FEEL SOMETHING, ANYTHING

Consumed by the unrelenting urge to feel something, anything, Jim cut himself with a razor blade. Shallow first, but progressively deeper the razor sliced his ashen flesh. Ritualistically he carved lines up and down his arms, legs, torso, and face. He gutted himself as a sacrifice for emotion, begging nothingness for something with his blood.

THE SOLUTION TO THE SCARECROW PROBLEM

This year, the crows descended upon the farmer's field as soon as the corn started producing little husk-heavy cobs, but the farmer could not afford any hay for a proper scarecrow until he had the money from the harvested corn.

The farmer crucified himself in the corn field, a scarecrow to protect his bountiful harvest.

MISOGYNISTIC TOASTER

Andy de Fonseca

SWEET CAROLINE

I knew she was dead but there she stood. Every night.

I used to scream, now I'm only annoyed. "How long will this go on?" I asked. She never spoke, just watched me from the end of the bed.

I killed her to make her go away, but now I see her more than ever.

ENTRY #1

april 17th
cheerios

do you want to know why i'm killing you, Cheerios? because eating you is like having sex with a barrel of hay. it's dry, even with milk. it's boring, even with a sugar cereal ratio of 5:1. fruit doesn't help, you lying fuck.

i'm going to enjoy killing you. it'll be... delicious.

ASS YOGA

Steve clenched his Gluteus Maximus and lifted the spoon, pulling himself into the ragdoll pose. He went down for a toe-stand dip and dunked the spoon. His pelvic floor twisted the spoon and got a heap of yogurt. He jerked into a downward dog and caught the yogurt in his mouth.

Julliard was not impressed.

LITTLE VICTORIES

There have been many debates regarding the issue. Countless social media polls. Nothing published in journals, but we all know we don't need a professional research team to verify the results. The naysayers are heathens, while those who accept and love are the chosen ones.

Now it's official. In print.

Pop-Tarts are better with butter.

IT'S ALL WET

Amber shivered, clutching Tim's coat. "I get it that all the old, racist men are dying. Things are getting better. But I'm getting older, too. At this point, I don't think I'll ever live in a world without all the hate."

Tim reached out. "Give me back my coat. You're getting sadness all over it."

OR... IS HE PART OF IT??

Did Bowser ever figure it out? Three original games. The first had eight worlds, each with four levels. The second, nine worlds, ten levels each. The third, eight worlds, at least six levels each. After all of that, did Bowser ever realize he was just part of a sexual game for Mario and Princess Peach?

IT WAS BEAUTIFUL

A mushroom cloud pulled up from earth like a massive volcano erupting. There was another, and another. And many more. The dark clouds spread, hiding more of the bright blue water Earth held. Large chunks broke off and floated into space.

"ISS to Mission Control, do you copy...? ISS to Mission Control, do you copy...?"

STUPID SHIT THAT'S BEEN SAID TO ME

"Are you sick?" I asked Tess outside of class.

"Just a weird cough," she answered. "They're the worst."

I nodded. "Sometimes I get this cough, but nothing comes out. Like, a silent cough."

"Ugh," some bitch listening scoffed. "I'm a smoker. I'm finding another way into class instead of listening to people make up coughs."

THERE'S THE PROBLEM

"I wish for immortality!"

Ellie's body tingled. She felt invigorated, youthful. The skies opened to every possibility.

And just as quickly, it passed. Apathy and boredom washed over her.

"Sort of takes the fun out of living," she said with dead eyes. "Everything you do is for the end point. I don't have that anymore."

STILL TOO SWEET

I emptied the salt bowl on my meal, but that didn't help. I fought a horse for his brick, but he won, so that didn't help. I went skinny dipping in Utah and got arrested. Certainly didn't help. I buried myself in Bolivia but a truck ran over me. Now I eat through a tube.

MY FRIEND, THE MANATEE

Frank the Manatee and I went swimming during a fiery sunset one summer evening. We ate some fish and crabs, raced with dolphins, dove into deep pools, played with a lady manatee's litter of calves.

"You know, Frank," I said, eating a fish sandwich, "I don't know much about you."

"No," Frank responded. "You don't."

ENTRY #7

may 1st
captain crunch

youve hurt so many others are you really surprised I came after you? even if the coppers caught me they wouldnt put me away. how many kids did you give bloody mouths? how many tears did they bitterly shed as they bit through the pain?

i'm doing the world a favor.

MILK IT

You will never be an actor. You suck at it. And you have a boring face.

They never believed in me.

Being a background actor isn't acting.

Yes, it is.

What part did you get, son? ...A tree? That's not acting.

I may be a tree... but I'll be the goddamned Sean Penn of trees.

I FOUND THIS AMULET...

The glowing red amulet promised a better life. My debt would disappear and I could finally eat without worry. The numbness in my arm would go away and I could use my hand again. I would find love.

"You rolled a one, critical fail."

As a fictional troll stole my amulet, my real worries remained.

IF A ZEBRA RAN THINGS

"Hey, Sheila, if you could change my one o'clock to two, that'd be super helpful. Thanks. Please remind marketing that we need those reports for OH SHIT FUCK SHIT FUCK A LION GOT IN HERE FUCKING SHIT SLUT HOW THE FUCK DID A FUCKING LION GET IN HERE SHIT SHEILA CALL THE FUCKING WRANGLER SHIT!"

SIMON'S EAR BONES

"Top of the morning, Malleus."

"Top of the morning, Incus. Pray, call me Hammer."

"I do beg your pardon, Hammer. Pray, call me Anvil."

"I do beg your pardon, Anvil. Top of the morning, Stapes."

"Top of the morning, Hammer. Pray, call me Stirrup."

"I do beg your pardon, Stirrup."

"Jolly good."

"Jolly good."

"Right-o."

OH, NO, IT'S DEAD AGAIN

"Shit shit shit."

A soft, persistent knock on the door reverberated throughout the room. "God? Are you okay?"

A sweat bead trailed down God's brow as he picked himself off the floor.

"Goooood? You in there, buddy...? Everyone's dead again."

God sighed. "Yeah... I'm here. Be right out."

He noted: *Move the Apocalypse button. Again.*

QUALITY CONTROL

An older woman answered the door. Her eyes were red, her hands shook.

"Good day, my name is Grim Reaper. I'm dropping by to see how your husband's death was. Do you believe he died in a fair, painless manner, or could his death have been tighter around the edges?"

She paused. "Tighter, I suppose."

THE FISH WHO WALKED UPRIGHT

"Herr derr, looker at me, I'm Evan. Derr I'ma walkin' upright. HERR DERR."

The surrounding fish laughed.

"Cut it out, guys!" Evan cried. "I'm still learning to swim!"

"Survival is thurr ability ta *adapt*, ya goldfish!"

Evan covered his eyes and wept. "I'm a trout."

"Ya gunna be *dinner* if ya don't fix your ways!"

PAPERS PLEASE

"Remove shoes and put your laptop in a bin."

Dave walked through the metal detector without a hitch.

"Sir, is this your bag?" Dave nodded. "Could you explain this, please?"

"Oh, that's just an external drive."

"Okay, thank you, sir. You're good to go. Have a safe trip."

And Dave had a rather pleasant flight.

LAST DAY OF WORK

Þ sat at his desk staring blankly at his parchment. The words stared back, reminding him of his obscurity.

"Heeeeey, buddy," T smiled. "How you holding up?"

Þ shrugged.

"Aren't you gone yet, douche?!" Y yelled over the cubicles. "Your desk is mine!"

"Fuck him." T patted Þ on the ascender. "He won't last long."

BONDING, BRAH!

HEY BRAHS! Ever been getting down and dirty with a hot piece? SURE YOU HAVE, BRAH. But she brings out a condom? Like, NO WAY, BRAH! Solution? Fake a LATEX ALLERGY, BRAH! In no time flat you can throw down with a mini brah that snagged your DNAs and shit. IT'S AMAZING, BRAH! Check it!

ENTRY #16

sept 20th
kix

i killed you slowly, as repayment for the eons i wasted trying to choke down your bland, insipid, vapid dry balls of chalk dust and air. you should have listened to your cousin, trix. trix not only went for flavor, but the ballsy fucker went for *shapes*.

you offered the world nothing.

STUPID SHIT THAT'S BEEN
SAID TO ME
PART 2

"Thanks for choosing Subway drive-through, how may I help you?"

"Burger, please."

"Sorry, sir, we only have subs."

"Ugh. Fine. What kind of subs?"

"Turkey, ham, chicken, meatball. The board shows all your options."

"I want fries."

"Sorry, sir, we have chips."

"What the hell? I want fries."

"McDonald's is right across the street, sir."

THE SUN IS TIRED

"Why does it rain, daddy?"

"That's just God crying for our sins, Emily."

"Why does it thunder, daddy?"

"That's just the clouds clapping for God's miracles, darling."

"Why is the sun getting closer, setting the trees afire, boiling our skin off our bodies, daddy?"

"That's just the sun going nap-nap, Emily, all in God's plan."

ASKED THE PRESIDENT

"I can't figure out which phrase to use."

"Depends on what you're modifying."

"Here, take a look-see."

He read. "Okay, is it a geeky lady with a boner? Or a lady with a geeky boner?"

She looked down. "Geeky boner."

"That means you're calling the boner a geek."

"Okay, I'll stick with 'geeky lady boner.'"

SUCK IT, LEWIS

I fell down

        the rabbit hole.

                It was under some
                    brush.

Down

            Down it goes.

      I pass by trinkets.
      Treasures

I reach for the drugs

              but I'm too slow.

      Down
        Down
          Down

I forget the sky.

My hands have wrinkles.

What awaits me

down there?

Down

Down

Down it goes

Where it stops, nobody

splat.

I READ THE INTERNET

Everyone is right, everyone is wrong, cats are the singularity, porn is the great peacemaker, knowing memes shows how cool you are, knowing memes shows how young you are, Facebook fights show how immature you are, there's no faith in humanity, everyone should have a trusted friend to delete your browser history upon your death.

Goose Jesus In:
ONE OF US

"And yea," the waterfowl's booming voice rang over the crowd, "thy god has sent me to deliver the holy word. Any *man* can claim to be the son of god. With me, thou shalt have no doubt of the divine."

Bruce mumbled to Jack. "When writing scripture, make some adjustments or we'll be laughed at."

MISSING UMBRELLA

Cory sighed as a computer mouse was dropped on the table. He grimaced as a toy soldier fell onto the floor. Next, a rubber dog toy and slender lotion bottle.

Cory tried to readjust his aching legs, but the stirrups held him in place.

The doctor grumbled. "It's like a fucking clown car down here."

GIVE THE DOG A BONE

Let me join you in the shower NO I DON'T WANT TO GET WET STOP Here throw my ball I SAID THROW MY BALL DON'T TAKE MY BALL Outside outside outside that's my favorite thing TREATS ARE MY FAVORITE THING NO CAR RIDES ARE MY FAVORITE THING I love you I LOVE THIS DEAD BIRD

TEETH

Having the dream of your teeth falling out usually means you have anxiety about something, or are feeling insecure, or have lost someone or something recently. It's never a good dream or feeling. However, what the hell does it mean when I dream about finding teeth and adding them to my mouth, and liking it?

HIGHER EDUCATION

Mrs. Premrose pointed her ruler to the chalkboard. "Rolling a pinner is quite rude if you have guests over. Start with a fattie to show good faith. If you want to get jolly, get a cross joint going. Absolutely *never* offer roaches. It shows you don't keep up on supply, and high society will know."

ENTRY #23

october 15th
frosted flakes

you thought you could hide from me. your brother got it and you knew your time was up. you're a sham, hidden by a coating of frost that masks your true intent:

to disintegrate into a puddle of slop as soon as you hit milk.

no one will care you're dead.

BAD THINGS HAPPENED

There's a small room in my soul I keep locked and hidden. Unlike the other places, this one contains a single feeling. I don't go looking for it, but occasionally it will find me. It pulls me in, the darkness seeps into me, and I must fight my way out.

It has only won once.

#HASHTAGFOREVERYTHING

#thanksgiving! #thanks #giving #food
#turkeyfood #turkeyisthebest #checkoutmyturkey
#ibaked #ibaketurkey #imacook! #ilovetocook
#mashedpotatoes #perfectturkey #corn
#cranberries #basted #bastedturkey #juicy
#perfectmeat #human #lol #silverservingplate
#turkeyhuman #bestpartofhuman #humanmeat
#pumpkinpie! #pumpkin #pilgrims #indians
#ribcage #husbandslol #cherrypie #sweetpotatoes
#sauce #hefitintheoven #butterrolls!
#musicoverscreams #redwine
#greenbeancasserole #familymeal #inlaws
#wheresrob? #glutenfree #matchingtablerings
#whenyoutrytonotpickatfoodbutitsdelicious
#gravy #mmmmgravy! #cleaneating
#marinateinbroth #businesstrip #nutrition
#foodie #fam #homesweethome #blessed

Goose Jesus In:
THICK AND THIN

Neil sat in a warm, humid, windowless room as Lucifer read over Neil's file. "I don't see anything here that explains your placement in Hell. Looks like you have led a pretty upstanding life and gave back to–" His eyes stopped on the bottom of the last page. He smirked. "Did you–did you really?"

CHASING THE DRAGON

"I'm not a fucking leprechaun, kid, back off." Herb the dragon whipped his tail that the young man kept slicing his sword across.

"Never!"

"Seriously, dick, that hurts."

"I shall destroy you for my lady, foul beAHHHH!"

CRUNCH.

"Play stupid games, win stupid prizes," Herb shrugged, dropping his jaws on a femur. "Like heroin addiction."

GENGHIS CAN'T

He ordered the creation of Mongol script, established religious freedom in his domain, united warring tribes, conquered almost all of the Eurasian Steppe, brought Eastern and Western civilizations into contact, and established a vast empire (killing around 40 million people in the process).

He did all of this, but couldn't stay on his damn horse.

COVERED BRIDGE

And all I can think of is, how did Adam and Barbara Maitland die from going over the side of a covered bridge?! Could they not open their doors and swim? Could they not hold their breaths for thirty seconds? The fall was a short distance, so no snapped necks happened. It doesn't make sense!

LYING ISSUES

“Did you remember the beer?”

“Yes.”

“Good. That guy called regarding that job you wanted. He said it was yours, but I told him we had to talk about it.”

“Alright.”

“You seem to be doing fine today. I told you: you didn’t have depression.”

“You were right.”

“That’s my girl. You love me.”

“Yes.”

CALCULATOR WATCH

Little Lucy tapped 5-9-1 into her watch. Shortly later a ground-shaking explosion sent fire into the sky.

“Lucy!” Her dad ran out the front door. “Thank goodness, you’re all right. I wonder what happened over there. What are you doing out here?”

Little Lucy smiled up at him, a G.I. Joe in her hand. “Playing.”

BANANA SCISSORS

Review: 1 star, Weak and Flimsy
By: Lorena B. on June 23, 1993

I tried using these tonight and they simply pinched the banana, instead of dicing it into several pieces in a quick, easy manner. I'll have to stick with a regular knife. Fast shipping, much appreciated.

Comment | 106,658 People found this review helpful.

FEELING BREAD

"They don't appreciate me," Trevor whined outside his office building. "I'm versatile, I can do anything they need. But it's too much. I'm strong on the outside, but inside? I'm all soft. I'm afraid I'm going to just harden to life, through and through."

"Yeah, man," said his sourdough bread bun. "I totally get it."

ENTRY #32

may 20th
corn flakes

i still don't know if every bowl i ate was stale or if that's just how you really taste. i never got corn flakes, i got corn dust. i would choke if i inhaled with a spoon close to my mouth. killing you was difficult. i think you were already dead.

Goose Jesus In:
RAISING THE STAKES

"Maverick! What the hell are you doing!"

The jet propelled through the air as the pilot closed his eyes. He clutched the dog tags. "Talk to me, Goose..."

"Come, follow me," Jesus said, "and I will–"

"*Cut!*"

A bell rang and assistants ran to restore the set.

"Damn it, Jesus, we talked about this!"

IT POPPED

I raced through the tall, damp grass with only the moonlight guiding me. The field was silent save for an animal calling out.

The top of the large, green globule came into view. Its skin was transparent, so earlier I was able to see something was moving inside.

But when I arrived, only tracks remained.

CHECKLIST

SUPPLIES FOR AWESOME PARTY:
1. Lots of balloons!
2. Chips, cookies, snacks, whatnot
3. Whiskey, raspberry vodka, mixers
4. See dealer for a dozen dime bags
5. Little umbrellas and stirrers, cherries
6. Rope / restraints
7. Tide pens
8. First Aid Kit
9. Whips, gags, floggers
10. Spreader bar
11. Wartenberg pinwheel
12. Piñata, candy

WORDS OF THE DYING

I'm ready. My family is around me and I've heard their last words, their love. There's my wife of sixty-two years, our three children, our eight grandchildren, and two great-grandchildren. The disease has taken my ability to talk, but not my ability to squeeze their hands. I curl my fingers to say, "I love you."

A LUMP IN TIME

"And if you look out the right of the ship you'll see the Cretaceous period, when dinosaurs had the most diversity. Further ahead you'll see Archimedes executing the first theoretical calculation using pi." The ship jumped, wobbled, and came to a halt. "I'm sorry for the inconvenience, we've hit something. We'll be back up shortly."

THEY KEEP THEM IN BARRELS

In three different companies around the world:

"How many barrels of whiskey were sold for this weekend?"

"Twenty-five, ma'am, right on target."

...

"Quick thinking, Jenkins! We just barely missed spilling 100,000 barrels of oil all over this coast."

...

"WHO LET THEM OUT? WHO LET THEM OUT? FOR THE LOVE OF GOD, THEY'RE THROWING SHIT EVERYWHERE."

"What's for dinner?"

"It's not like we have much of a choice."

"Well, if *someone* would go out searching like the others..."

"Fuck you, Steve, I know you're talking about me."

"Could you assholes put your differences aside and *try* having sex?"

"I don't care if he's the last white rhino on earth, he nasty."

COACH

"Coach Coach on Coach! Coach Coach on Coach! Coach Coach on Coach!"

More suburban moms parked their Highlanders outside the school and lifted signs.

"Coach Coach on Coach! My kid deserves a classy leader!"

"Coach Coach on Coach! I'm embarrassed by your Wal-Mart handbag!"

"Coach Coach on Coach! Honestly, where are my tax dollars going!"

I HAVE NO IDEA WHAT'S GOING ON

Thoughts throughout my life:

"Yellow? What? What's a square?"

"Yay! I made the basketball team! How do I play this sport?"

"LOL sin cos what, math?"

"Okay, so... just pay minimum on student loans?"

"This job calls for reports and I don't know what an excel is."

"So, this 'baby' needs to be watched constantly?"

SCARED OF NOTHING

Nothing is an absence of something. So, what happens after you die?

Nothing.

What do you feel after you die?

Nothing.

Must be something? A color, a noise, a different sense.

Nothing.

In a dark room, close your eyes, plug your ears. That's still something. Death is nothing. You don't even notice. You're just gone.

DREAMS OF FUTURES PAST

DJ Tyrer

I
The Message

THE CAVE
(I)

A figure in a cave, crouched over a codex, reed pen scratching words upon vellum. The thoughts he records are not his own. They torment his dreams and linger amongst his waking thoughts, prompting him, demanding he record them, empty his mind of their unwholesome presence.

Finally, he finishes the tome, and passes it on.

THROUGH MANY AGES

Through many ages that tome is passed down, copied, rewritten, amorphous yet always the same. It speaks of things that have happened, that will happen, that never happened and, yet, are happening now.

To read it is to become part of it, nothing more than a character in its plot, thinking the thoughts it contains.

THE ANTIQUARY

The antiquary lusts for a certain book to add to his collection. It's all he desires.

Then, it comes into his possession: to gain it, he had to do terrible things.

His conscience aches as he reads its fragile pages.

Then he finds himself repeating the words it contains.

He's found in his shop—murdered.

THE YELLOW SIGN

"Tell me, have you seen the Yellow Sign?"

"The Yellow Sign?"

"Yes, the Yellow Sign. Have you seen it?"

"I have seen it in my dreams and drawn upon the pavement in crumbly chalk. But, tell me, have you? Have you seen the Yellow Sign?"

"No, never. I seek one to show me."

"Then, look..."

I DREAMT AGAIN

"I dreamt again of the city of yellow sandstone and illicit love."

"Speak not of that place. It is not real, and if it were... its existence would doom us all."

"I know, and yet I long to dwell there beneath the light of the twin suns."

"It is not real."

"Look out the window."

DOOMSDAY

He sees a vision of a world engulfed in devastation. A blazing red sun scalding away its atmosphere, evaporating its oceans till not even thin mists remain. Life fades away.

And, through it all, a figure clad in red wanders, lions licking its hands; it bows before a yellow-robed King.

He tries to warn them.

THE MADMAN

The madman has a message. If only they would listen, heed his warnings.

He has foreseen the end, but they do not care. When he speaks of the book, they merely laugh at him.

In his dreams he conceives a plan. Or, was the plan handed to him?

He shall cleanse the world. He alone.

THE KILLINGS

Hastur—the word is smeared on the mirror in lipstick.

"What does it mean?" asks the uniformed officer as he turns back to the body on the bed.

The detective shrugs. "A person, a place, a possibility..."

"This is the third killing like this," says the CSI. "We'll soon have them."

The detective shudders. "Maybe."

MURDER

A bloodied knife plays host to a sense of power. He caresses the sticky blade as if making love to it. It is part of his soul.

A list of names declares those he must kill if he is to achieve absolution. The last name is his own.

Only a few more left to go.

THE GREEN ROOM

He comes offstage to rapturous applause and enters the green room, wiping vigorously at his face to remove the greasepaint. He looks up, exclaims—bodies are scattered about and blood's splashed up the walls. They're all dead.

He awakes sweating, a knife clutched to his chest, the taste of blood on his lips.

He smiles.

THE STRANGER

A late-night knock at the door. Instinct tells her not to answer, but she does.

A stranger, the skin of his face wan and waxen like a mask, stands upon the step.

"Yes?" she asks, nervous.

No answer, he merely holds out a package.

She takes it, unwraps it: a book.

Looks up; he's gone.

THE BOOK

The book sits on her bedside table for several days before she dares open its mustard covers and begin to read it. A play. She has never read a play before, yet finds it strangely compelling. She reads through the night

Sleep creeps up on her and her eyes slowly shut. She begins to dream.

THE BALL

She finds herself playing a part amongst the throng at a ball, each one masked—a player, not a person.

A figure, taller than the rest, strides through their midst; the guests recoil.

Then, come midnight, the hour is struck and the call goes out to unmask.

"I wear no mask."

"No mask? No mask!"

ANXIETY

Strange dreams. Nightmares. Night terrors wrench her from her sleep.

Soon, she finds she cannot sleep at all, too anxious to relax, half-remembered thoughts gnawing at her soul. She wonders if she can go on.

She faces a choice: embrace the fear or end it all.

She reaches for a blade, picks up the book.

LOVERS

The blonde women could be sisters in matching yellow dresses.

Their eyes met across the crowded bar and one crossed to the other and sat beside her. No words were exchanged; they merely slipped their arms around each other, their lips meeting in a tantalising kiss.

Camilla and Cassilda pledged to meet again in Carcosa.

THE DRESS

The detective picks up the evidence bag and stares at its contents: a yellow dress, marred by a brown stain of blood. He thinks back to the victim, a beautiful young woman, and the dichotomy of how vivacious she still appeared despite her pallid-mask face.

He remembers her father, devastated at her death.

So sad.

MANY MOONS

Camilla wakes from dreams of Cassilda to a room filled with ivory moonlight. She rises and crosses to the window. Where there should be one moon, there are many crowding the midnight sky.

Something flaps languidly across the faces of the orbs. She stifles a scream. It swoops down towards her. She tries to run.

WILFUL CREATURES

She loved cats. Wilful creatures: they do as they please, without regard for human desires or demands. They stay as long as it suits them and leave when they wish.

At night, she watches in her dreams as the cats dance their way heavenward towards the many moons overhead.

She longs to follow them thence.

CAT'S EYES

Absently, her hand moved rhythmically, stroking its soft, warm back to the accompaniment of its purr. She found it calming to caress it.

Yet, when the room was bright with moonlight, it would sometimes hiss and stare at a corner. She could see no-one there.

But, sometimes, she heard the swish of a tattered robe.

MISSING

Cats love to wander, in this world and in dream, coming and going as they desire.

One day, her favourite didn't return—from where, she didn't know.

She knocks on all the doors in the block, speaks to those few neighbours who answer. None know where it went.

But paths begin to converge in consequence.

CONVERGENCE

Two separate lives converge for a brief, tantalising period. Camilla speaks to her upstairs neighbour and suggests certain volumes he might wish to read.

He entertains notions of romance, not knowing her heart belongs to another, an unobtainable desire. He begins to read, hoping to please her, only to corrupt his dreams. He goes mad.

DREAMLANDS

She dreams, drifting past curious vistas until she arrives in a strange land in a tornado of fire. Before her, a roadway of lemon hue.

A voice says, "Follow the yellow brick road."

She walks that path to a city: sapphire yellow, not emerald; home to a King, not a wizard. She names it *Carcoza*.

CARCOZA

The King offers her His hospitality: a week in the dreamy Yellow City to enjoy its decadent delights. She takes lover after lover, only to feel disgust in the morning's golden light as she recalls the way they squirmed against her like worm-ridden corpses.

She sips yellow wine to dull such thoughts before taking another.

THE LAMIA

The Great and Powerful Carcoz speaks and she listens, a tingle of ecstasy rising into a flood. His words arouse and nauseate her.

He sends her forth from His Yellow City to the night-haunted west to kill a lamia.

She confronts it without weapons, only a symbol: a sign of His power.

It is her.

AWAKENING

She wakes from dream with an agonised scream.

Memory fades, leaving only shadows.

Did she—could she—kill herself?

Yes, she could, if only death would reunite her with the one she loves.

She takes a knife and lays it against her wrist, only to hesitate.

Slowly, she presses down.

A trickle, then a flood.

ALONE

He sits alone, touching the cool knife to his flesh. The sting is comforting.

It's over. His task is done. Just one last name remains upon the list.

If only he had the nerve.

Even now, self-preservation begs at his resolve.

"It is a terrible thing..." he murmurs, a tear in his eye.

It's over.

II
Preparations

AREA 51

"Area 51 is nothing more than an urban myth," the officer tells the assembled journalists.

Behind the razor-sharp fence, teams of scientists assemble to be vouchsafed secrets no-one in authority wishes the public to know.

"It can see my dreams! It can see my dreams!"

The room is sealed, the scientist locked away. He dreams.

SLUGABED

In a room with blank walls, laid upon a mattress, itself laid upon the floor, he dreams. Sometimes, when awake, he reads the same book over and over with a quiet obsession. Sometimes, he just stares at the wall or the floor, reliving his dreams. In his dreams, he is free, soaring amongst the stars.

THE DREAM

The project was the dream of one man, now forgotten. He became an embarrassment and had to be locked away. Nobody wanted to know him once he went mad. Nobody wanted to acknowledge the fact he drew his wild ideas from ancient, mouldering tomes, not shiny, cutting-edge science, nor that those ideas drove him mad.

CALCULATIONS

The numbers are unnerving, not of this Earth. They describe a reality that cannot be perceived by human senses, a whole new vision of space-time.

Mathematicians work hard to crack the secrets of this science that will propel a vessel to another world.

Finally, one comprehends the equation. Success!

He is never the same again...

HOPE

He agrees to join the project, not for self-aggrandisement nor for scientific zeal, but out of a hidden kernel of hope, hidden deep in his soul.

After his daughter was murdered, he imagined life held nothing more for him. Then, hope was kindled at the thought: in distant regions of space, even death may die.

DEVELOPMENTAL PHASE

The development phase takes years. The calculations were merely the first stage. Now, they must build the vessel that will carry them through strange angles of space-time. Security is tight, but still rumours leak out, finding fertile ground in the more paranoid corners of the internet. Stories of madness and an apocalypse are firmly denied.

LIGHT SPEED

Traditional physics limits the speed of spacecraft, but new geometries allow exceptions to the rule by side-stepping that limitation. A thousand mathematicians have worked for years to calculate the formulae necessary for the trip. Now, the captain inputs the command code and the computer does the rest, warping space-time and opening the gate to Aldebaran.

III
En Route

SPACESHIP

The vacuum of space allows options of size and shape unavailable within an atmosphere, and momentum negates the need for fuel expenditure between launch and arrival, leading to a gothic city of spires undertaking the journey through space. A crew of thirteen has acres each to live in, but cluster nonetheless. Empty corridors echo strangely.

SPACESUITS

They practice regularly. The spacesuits are the very best available, a dozen generations better than those used on the moon. Flexible, hardened against radiation and micro-meteors, filled with redundant fail-safes, they cannot fail.

Suddenly, an alarm, shrill in his ear. The HUD flashes yellow, a peculiar symbol. He screams. Then, it's gone and silence falls.

THE RED EYE

It haunts their dreams: a blazing red eye gazing down upon them from the distant horizon, judging and finding them wanting.

"I had the weirdest dream last sleep cycle."

"Me, too."

He proceeds to describe it, she interrupts with details. They stare at each other in confusion, fear. The Red Eye: what does it mean?

SHIP'S CAT

The scientists hadn't been too pleased at the request, but she had been insistent.

"Every ship deserves its cat," she said, and they shrugged and said, "Sure."

It would pace the corridors as the vessel drifted through the darkness, sometimes keeping them company and sometimes keeping its own counsel.

But, when she dreamed, it flew.

DARK STAR

The stars in this sector don't shine with light, but express a darkness. Frozen stars, collapsed into gateways to the world of the dead. The discoverers stand transfixed at the sight, their human minds incapable of comprehending the contrasts between what they seem to perceive and what actually *is*. Some will never recover their minds.

THE DEAD

They dream of the dead. They see them in their dreams, in places they once knew; and in waking moments, silhouetted against bulkheads or upon computer screens. Some they recognise: loved ones, friends, colleagues who died to get them this far.

Then there are the others, human yet *not* human.

All bring a message: *Doom.*

LOVED ONE

She comes to him in his dreams: his daughter, dead so many years. Haunted eyes, bloodstained yellow dress. She whispers something his ear cannot quite catch—a name? A warning? A verse from the Bible? A passage from a play?

"Stay with me," he begs, but she silently turns away, crumbles, and scatters like dust.

IV
Destination

ALDEBARAN

They reach their destination, the great red star that's haunted their dreams since they set out: Aldebaran.

They survey the system: there are planets. A world with a thin atmosphere attracts their attention. Numerous moons swirl about it in a wild ballet.

Preparations are made for them to approach it, explore it, discover its secrets.

ORBIT

They leave the ship at the edge of the system and move in-system aboard the orbiter, which will be their base of operations. They halt several world diameters out to avoid the many moonlets that circle the planet.

They prep their drones and satellites and send them out to map the red-lit world.

They wait.

THE PLANET

Red-lit wastelands stretch to a bloodstained horizon, scattered with the wind-worn remains of aeon-old cities. A flurry, a movement. The drone swoops lower, attracted by the anomaly. Reality, or an artefact of pixels and swirling dust? A yellow figure momentarily silhouetted against the red sands. Then, nothing. Stillness. Will an operator even notice the scene?

THE RUINS

There are ruins here, a hint of a city hidden beneath ancient sands. The drone swoops back and forth, mapping the site and sending up images that cause consternation. This evidence of sentient life is unexpected; officially, at least. None of them are willing to discuss the dreams they've had, the fact they recognise it.

THE CITY

There was a city here once, vibrant with life and culture. They dream themselves back to lives there, their own or others infecting them. The streets filled with wonders with towers that seemed to soar up past the many moons in the sky.

A masked ball. All attend.

A stranger.

They awake before the end.

LANDFALL

Ruddy sands explode upwards in clouds as retro-rockets fire, cushioning their landing.

They wait for the sands to settle, revealing the flat, unrelenting wasteland, then descend the ramp, the first people on a new world.

They approach the ruins, cautious and curious in equal measures. Seven enter, but one will not return, his fate unknown.

THE SEARCH

How can a man just vanish into thin air?

They move swiftly through those ruins of some elder age, seeking a sign, then retreat defeated. The radio waves are silent of his voice.

The ruins are declared off limits. Perhaps there are some things humanity is not meant to know. Yet, he haunts their dreams.

FOOTPRINTS

As they explore, they are surprised to find a line of parallel indentations in the red-lit sands: footprints. Footprints that do not belong to any of the seven of them. Someone else is on this world with them...

They follow the tracks in both directions and halt, confused. They begin suddenly and end the same.

RADIO WAVES

"Hello? Hello?"

Something about the planet disrupts their radios. Sometimes they are silent, save for odd crackles and screeches. Sometimes unfamiliar voices seem to whisper wordlessly, sometimes calling their names.

Then, there are those fragments:

"It is..."

"...a terrible thing..."

Repeated over and over with menace, if no clear meaning.

The mission leader starts sobbing.

MADNESS

They gather together in the capsule in a state of agitation.

"We must leave—we must leave!"

"Have you seen the Yellow Sign?"

"It sleeps beneath the lake, dreaming."

"No mask? No mask!"

"We must leave—we must leave!"

The mission leader attempts to restore order, but cannot be heard.

"It is a terrible thing..."

REBIRTH

He sees her on a distant hill. At first, she's nothing but a silhouette amidst a swirl of dust. He moves closer and grows certain: it's her.

He approaches her, reaches out and hugs her, the daughter he hasn't seen for so many lonely years. Scalloped rags enfold him. He screams as his helmet cracks.

SANDSTORM

Winds whip up the red-hued sands, engulfing them in a swirling chaos. Figures seem to move through the sands, encircling them. Sometimes they draw close, almost touching them. At others, they move away, beckoning.

"Mum, is that you?"

"Darling?"

They do not respond, just beckon.

Then a taller figure sweeps by, clad in swirling robes.

EXPLORATION

Somehow she has become separated from the others. The radio is useless, just whispers. Still, she can keep on exploring until they locate her.

Sandstone columns might be natural, shaped by the wind, yet hint at some ancient colonnade. She pauses to take photos.

Then she sees him: a figure in a yellow scalloped robe.

MANTRA

They find her hours later, a drone having located her and beamed them her coordinates. When they reach her, she is sitting against a sandstone column, trembling. A check reveals her oxygen levels are fine.

She repeats words over and over: "It is a terrible thing to fall into the hands of the Living God."

THE CAVE
(II)

They walk across the red-lit wastes towards a cave, their forms bulky in their vacuum suits. Warily, they step into the dark interior; torch beams illuminate shafts through the blackness.

"Look," crackles a voice across radio waves. A gloved hand gestures to a corner.

A figure sits, long dead, mummified, a book upon its lap.

THE TASTE OF SAND ON YOUR LIPS

Betty Rocksteady

YOU SHOULDN'T BE HERE

Maybe if you got here sooner. But you're here *now*, aren't you? There's nothing I can do about it. You keep turning pages, greedy, eating words like berries, red juice spilling down your chin. It's disgusting. It's obsessive. You should stop. Leave. Don't come back.

I guess it's too late.

You really shouldn't be here.

THE PLANET IS AN OCEAN

The ocean is dead. Rumors say it was never alive at all. The water reflects black skies, deep and dark and thick. The sea is still as a tomb, but for the occasional lapping wave that licks the island, a vicious tongue, swallowing grains of sand, kissing the shores with its poison.

No one swims.

THE ISLAND APPEARS

It might be a mirage. When you blink, it seems to disappear.

For now, it is fiercely alive, writhing with motion, with things that play and scream and fuck and devour and sleep. Beginnings, middles, ends.

The island gives way, bit by bit. Soft sand dissolves to ocean. It has been here forever. It endures.

THE EYE

Huge and throbbing, blinded in a long ago war. Milk white, buried deep in the forest. You walk by, so quiet, afraid it can hear. It blinks and squints and tears drip silently to the ground, burning grass and weeds, turning insects to muck.

Once all-seeing, once all-knowing, now afraid. And so you pass, unobstructed.

THERE ARE NO FISH IN THE OCEAN

Clouds spill to feed the island. Pink-stained fog coughs and spits out a fish. He lands on his feet, his breath coarse and ragged.

A child offers him a glass of water. He dives in. She places him on a bench and forgets.

His memory lasts fifty-five seconds, then he forgets, too.

He is content.

AT THE CROSSROADS

The King leaves the castle. He has heard those distant rumblings. It is dangerous, but he goes alone. His court no longer listens to him. He wants more than this. There are answers to find.

The cats sit at the crossroads, cleaning their paws. They have no advice for him.

He makes the wrong choice.

THE SIAMESE-SIAMESE CATS

A single tail that twists and winds. Flashing eyes. Whiskers flicker with impatience. Rough tongue reassures.

"How long shall we stay?"

"Until it's over."

"And when will it be over?"

"Soon, brother, soon."

"And how will we escape?"

"A way will open."

"It always does."

A yawn. They curl together. No point in losing sleep.

THE TEETH

Chattering clattering teeth, gnash and spit and chew. Pearly whites made of clouds, what they eat is left behind.

Just stay still. It doesn't hurt. Let them pass you by.

Watch them! They tear at your heels and gnaw their way through, but you don't feel a thing. They go on and so do you.

MOTHER

Her belly expands and contracts. She feeds it handfuls of dirt, crunchy beetles. She gulps puddle water. There is no one left to ask for advice.

She has no idea how long it takes.

It has been years. It has been longer.

She has torn off her face and sewn it to her gut, waiting.

THE HAPPY CLOWN

No one has seen the clown for years, but you can visit him if you want. He's in The Queen's dungeon. She doesn't know he's there. You don't need a key, the door is open. He is not trapped. He just remains.

Melted face, white and red and dead. He smiles.

He is not missed.

THE SKY GROWS STRANGE

Don't look up. Don't look up. Don't look up. Don't look up. Don't look up. Don't look up. Don't look up. Don't look up. Don't look up. Don't look up. Don't look up. Don't look up. Don't look up. Don't look up. Don't look up. Don't look up. Don't look up. Don't look up. Don't look up. Don't.
Something is coming.

THE EARTH IS SHAKING

Don't look down. Don't look down. Don't look down. Don't look down. Don't look down. Don't look down. Don't look down. Don't look down. Don't look down. Don't look down. Don't look down. Don't look down. Don't look down. Don't look down. Don't look down. Don't look down. Don't look down. Don't look down. Don't.
Something is coming.

THE HUNT FOR THE KING

Where did The King go? He has been gone for a long time, and something distant is rumbling.

We send armies of ants to retrieve him. They scatter across the island, tiny legs stiff but fast. They find nothing. They find no one.

Everyone wakes up at once. Everyone looks. There is nothing to find.

LONG LIVE THE QUEEN

The Queen is dead. She was sewing her mouth together when the needle slipped and plunged deep into her heart. Out spurted a ribbon, jagged and purple and thick. She grew light-headed. There was no chance to save her. She fell from the tower, tangled and strangled in her own blood.

We watched it happen.

THE WORM WAKES

Beneath the earth it churns. Each undulation shifts tiny cities of sand and lays them to waste. A timid head pokes out from the ground, unseeing, seeking, not finding.

Something about it bothers you deeply. You pluck it from its hole and throw it to the fish.

The fish eats and forgets. You do not.

THE HUT

Rock and clay and moss sunk deep in the muck, far past the desert, where no one goes.

Rumors say an old god lived there, back when rumors said anything at all. Now the gods are dead. Only we remain.

The door cracks open. Something dark and low and oily slithers out. No one sees.

THE ADVERSARIES

Their battle dragged on for five hundred and fifty-five years. They grew bloodied and bruised beyond repair, but still they fought on. Legs quivered but held.

The sun turned black. They were distracted. They looked up.

They were not blinded, yet it was the last thing they ever saw.

One reached for the other's hand.

THE SAD CLOWN

He is crying. He never stops crying. Hidden beneath the castle, he felt when she died. We all did.

Melted face, soggy candle. Wax and blood and greasepaint stain the concrete. The door yawns open. He can leave anytime. He stays. He cries.

He would escape if there was anything left of him to run.

HE KEEPS ON MOVING

The King journeys to places unseen. The woods part to take him further and close behind him. The trees display new colors, vivid and impossible on this grey island. Miraculous visions appear to him, clarifying nothing.

He is confused. He stumbles forward. He stumbles back. He is pushed along, a swimmer in a dangerous current.

HOW MANY LEGS DOES THE OCTOPUS HAVE?

He lurks on the top of the mountain. Bulbous head extends into the sky, shimmering clouds obscure his view.

His legs are long and tapered, branching off into twists and thorns, reaching to all the secret places of the sands, touching everything. They caress and pinch, squeezing blood from stones. He knows all, says nothing.

THE MAN IN THE CLAY HOUSE

He's almost done, so he starts again. He won't finish. What happens after you finish? It worries him. So when the end comes, he stops, rips it up, starts over. It's easier to begin and begin than it is to start something different. He works quicker each time. He tears up. He tears it up.

THEY TORE EACH OTHER APART

When news of her death came, neither sister shed a tear. The older arched her brow. "I'm next in line."

"But I'm the smartest and prettiest."

"Perhaps, but I am the oldest."

"I am faster."

"I am stronger," and she was upon her little sister.

She lied. They were well matched.

There was no winner.

IN A THIMBLE

The water is still, not even a ripple, until the mermaids rise. They are not beautiful. They are full of teeth, each scale a mouth, and each mouth starving. When they wake, they scream. They used to sing, but their voices are hoarse. The King hears them and he stays away.

He is still lost.

THE CATS GROW WORRIED

They prowl and pace, unable to assuage their fears by grooming. They don't know what is coming, just that it is strong and fierce and comes and comes.

"I think I'm hungry."

"You just ate."

"Did I? Perhaps."

The fish closes his eyes and they pass him by.

"We must keep walking."

And they do.

EVERYONE WAKES UP

At exactly the same time. No clock strikes, but our eyes all blink open. We are blind for a moment, unaccustomed to the light.

A heavy sense of dread fills your heart, and mine. The taste of blood floods your mouth. It is time.

You look to the sky and see nothing.

I'm so sorry.

WORD HAS SPREAD

The wind is whispering. The leaves are falling. Everyone knows, but no one remembers how they heard. Somewhere in the distance, a dog screams. The eye falls from the sky, careens through the sand. The clown is laughing and laughing and laughing. I am picking flesh from my thumb. I told you not to come.

A DOOR APPEARS

A rough sketch appears on the horizon. Hazy brushstrokes are refined, it bursts into three dimensions. Lines are sketched, finalized, inked. Next, a wash of color is applied. Plain mahogany shifts and changes into something exquisitely carved. With each moment that passes, new details come into view. A brass door knob bulges. A keyhole gapes.

THE OCEAN STIRS

These waters have always been dead and dark and empty. But now, leagues and leagues below where the water meets the sky, something massive wakes.

It yawns, stretches, and adjusts its bulk into a more comfortable position. Eyes blink shut. It falls back into a dying dream.

Above, the seas are rough. The waves climb.

EVERYONE WANTS TO BE THE QUEEN

Bushes rustle, trees fall. Everyone is dying. We are all out for blood. Some of us rage and run and scream. Some of us sneak, lay traps, move in shadows. Something grinds against the sky.

Days pass and the dead are walking.

They chew and chew and chew and chew.

Everyone has a master plan.

MAPS DON'T WORK HERE

The girl rips hers apart, piece by piece. Faded mountains, crusted rivers, beloved homes; a mess of jagged melodrama. She wipes tears on dusty plains. The wind picks up. She scatters it to the sky.

She starts on herself. Paper face, paper fists, paper heart drift into the breeze.

A sliver of mouth whispers, "Goodbye."

STOP WHAT YOU'RE DOING

Jam your fingers into your eardrums. Deeper. Ignore the pain. Hum. Concentrate on your breath. Close your eyes and start counting. Think of a safe place, somewhere far away. Farther. Keep humming. Keep counting.

When you feel my hand on your shoulder, it's safe.

If you count to fifty-five and don't feel my hand, run.

THE SISTERS

A nose, an eye, a lock of hair.

A hand, a cheek, a hunk of lung.

Blood attacks vein. Bone attacks nail. A tongue strangles an intestine, a toe is severed by teeth. Eyeballs roll like dice, fingers fall like dominos.

A puzzle of body parts, each scrap of flesh in its own private war.

THE RAGE OF STARS

Night falls then falls again, darker. The sky swirls with crimson, an inky Rorschach.

You can't see them, but you can hear them. Each star has a tiny mouth and they are screaming.

Black waves are churning, building tall and fast and strong.

You pick stardust from your hair, so sharp it cuts your fingers.

BREAKFAST

He refuses and pushes the bowl away.
"Eat your porridge, it's your favorite kind."
He frowns, pale face solemn.
"If you don't eat, you won't grow big and strong."
His voice is static, out of tune, not human.
"There is no survival. This is the end."
His mother shakes her head, then bites his off.

THE WITCH ON THE HILL

She is singing a song you haven't heard in a long time. Her voice hurts something buried deep within you, forces you to remember. Hearts pulse, wings tear, vocal cords sever. The thing inside you dies.

Even the hill shrivels away, a sunken valley. The witch becomes stone, then dust.

I don't like this song.

A KEY IS FOUND

"It's coming."

"Of course it is. I told you that."

"How much time?"

"Barely any."

"Then what shall we do?"

"We wait. First, we eat."

Ears slant back. A rustle, a pounce, a spray of blood. Hunger sated. Within the belly of the mouse, it glitters, plucked free with razor teeth.

"Well, that's a relief."

THE WOODS

The trees carve eyes into their trunks so they can watch. Gnarled folds hiss. Ropey branches twine together like the king of rats. They clench and release, clench and release. Something whines. Blood drips to the forest floor. On the breeze, the scent of burnt flesh.

The squirrel slices his belly open and sacrifices himself.

THE SALT PICKS AWAY AT EVERYTHING

The sky opens and showers us with salt. Our voices are too hoarse to scream. Stinging grains exfoliate as they peel back the surface of the land. Twin cats press close together beneath a mountain of garbage, listening to the sizzle of slugs.

It rains for a time, then stops.

We all display new flesh.

PUSH BACK

The warriors stamp their feet, tear down walls, open gates. Glass overflows, water splashes, fish goes belly up. The clown is exposed to the elements. The mermaids eat, something silky stains their teeth. The pregnant gut explodes, the baby crawls, the mother screams:

WHERE IS THE KING WHERE IS THE KING WHERE IS THE KING?

THE WAVES

The ocean is black and oily and thick. The water beneath the surface is chaos. The water above the surface is a war. Waves crash together like angry thunder. The stars fall and sink and fade.

THE OCEAN IS DEAD THE OCEAN IS DEAD THE OCEAN IS DEAD.

The waves scream and shake and growl.

DON'T LOOK, THE MOON IS SMILING

Fat and heavy, hanging low enough to touch. Wicked teeth extend past cheeks, chewing stars and clouds. The lemmings look up (the sky is falling). They are destroyed in flame. The moon laughs, a cold breeze, and even their ashes disappear.

He turns his head, crumples the sky.

Close your eyes, he wants a kiss.

DIZZY SPELLS

They are spinning and spinning and spinning. Each mouth is agape in rictus grin. The sickness makes their eyes bulge wide.

They dance in tandem. Their shoes wear thin. Soft, delicate feet bleed where the leather frays—a trail of blood that leads back to a shattered home.

They are spinning and spinning and spinning.

ROCK MOUNTAIN

A child sits on her swing set. Deep in shadow, her mother plucks weeds.

The swing stops. "Do you hear that?"

"Yes." Her mother turns in slow motion, her face is not her own. A puppet string lifts a shell to her ear.

Beneath their feet, the earth opens. The mountain crumbles. They are gone.

THE MAN WITH THE SUITCASE

He is crouched beneath a tree, cradling a tattered suitcase. His long fingers are tied in complex knots around the handle. Black blood drips from his ear and stains his white suit.

He shakes. He gathers his nerve and opens the case. The wicked winds blow, the contents escape.

There is no hope. Not here.

TOO FAR GONE

The seams of the sky groan. Trees pull away from the ground and march off on broken branches. The earth patches itself up, but soil falls through the cracks.

Everything is falling apart. The armies of ants sew it back together, but their needles are dull and rusted. Their thread is too thin. It tears.

A DOOR IS USED

At last they arrive.

"I was beginning to think we wouldn't find it."

"Where shall we head to next?"

The key slides home. "An excellent question, brother."

The door sighs open. They hesitate on the threshold, but the wind hisses a melody, and even a cat must decide quickly.

The door shuts behind them, disappears.

I HEARD SOMEONE CRYING

Cover your ears. You'll thank me later.

The banshees are out. They circle the sky like vultures, snatch children from the sand. Their necks are brittle, heads twist off with a snap.

Many have already given up. All through the village, face down in the sand, they take their fingers from their ears and bleed.

TOO LATE

The King stumbles through the sand, sees a familiar curve of tree. Everything clicks. He knows where he is; he knows the way home.

No one cheers for him. The beach is empty.

He turns to the castle, to where it should be. A dark, oily stain hangs in the sky.

He hears himself whimper.

I SMELL SOMETHING ON THE WIND

Do you smell it, too? Salty. Rotten. Meaty. Dead and burning. A pyre of garbage and spoiled flesh.

Nothing looks the same anymore. The sun is a scribble. The sky is a mouth. Everyone is on fire, but it blinks in and out.

Ashes, ashes.

I am so afraid for the fire to go out.

THE HORRIBLE SOUND OF SILENCE

Everything stops dead. A distant hum cuts off abruptly. Hundreds of eyes look to each other for comfort. Pupils dilate, enormous holes that lead to the sky. In that darkness, unholy stars swirl.

Your mouth is moving. I can't hear you. All our mouths are moving, thousands of teeth grinding silent.

Tears are razor sharp.

CRASHING WAVES

The storm started so long ago that it became commonplace.

The water crashes against the sand, no longer sated by just a taste, hungry for more, licking faster and further up the shore, taking great gulps of people and the places they called home. No one screams. Not anymore.

The ocean is dead and starving.

TSUNAMI

The entire ocean sighs. THE GREAT WAVE is coming. It eclipses what is left of the sky. It eclipses *everything*.

It is so fucking beautiful.

Everywhere I look, all I see is ocean.

I smell death in her waves.

Everyone left standing sinks to their knees.

No one prays.

This *is* God. God is here.

THE FORCE OF THE OCEAN

Rock, paper, scissors, the sea. The ocean always wins. Greedy, she swallows us whole. Everything is death.

I don't know which way is up. Wicked waters displace and destroy.

The taste of blood in your mouth mingles with the taste of sand on your lips.

Everything sinks slowly in these black waters.

Goodbye, goodbye, goodbye.

THE DROWNING

No one can swim.

There is nowhere to run, there is nowhere to hide. The island is devoured. We are devoured. Waves scatter our remains.

Time passes.

Eventually, the waters smooth. Not a grain of sand is left untouched. For a short time, bodies bob on the surface, then they sink.

There is nothing left.

ALL IS QUIET

All is still.

It's just the two of us. I'm sorry I can't meet your gaze, but you could have stopped this at any time. *I* could have stopped this at any time.

We have to live with our choices.

We will go on. We will to try to forget.

Please, just turn the page.

ABOUT THE AUTHORS

Stephanie M. Wytovich is the Poetry Editor for Raw Dog Screaming Press, and her Bram Stoker Award-nominated poetry collections, *Hysteria: A Collection of Madness*, *Mourning Jewelry*, and *An Exorcism of Angels* can be found at www.rawdogscreaming.com. Her debut novel, *The Eighth*, will be out in early 2016 from Dark Regions Press. Follow Wytovich at: stephaniewytovich.blogspot.com

"**Michael Allen Rose**" consists of the set of the first three words in this paragraph. "This" is the fifteenth word in the paragraph; however, it is actually the first word of the second sentence. It is imperative that you understand that "it" is also the way in which the author chose to begin this, the third sentence of this bio, and also the most complex sentence of the paragraph, considering that "it" is also the twenty-fifth, thirty-fifth, forty-second and seventy-second word. Michael enjoys being metafictional, subjective, droll, and formally experimental. These are some of the root causes that might explain his annoying tendency to create metafiction even in his own biographical information, which is symptomatic of pretensions and deep-seated mental illness.

A new paragraph begins here, utilizing a

present tense construct to emphasize the textual fluidity and unpredictability of the biographical information. In the next sentence, the author will engage directly with the reader in order to bring some sort of reflective nature to the idea of reading this biography. Would you classify this as fiction or non-fiction? The reader cannot answer the question for the author, only for themselves, thus making this an exercise in futility. Also, the amusing construction of this bio—an attempt at humor by an obviously delusional writer—has not used the word "it" since the counting of the word in the paragraph above. Of course, by calling attention to that, the author has completely disrupted the attention of the reader by ruining the flow of the piece, not to mention that it is likely the poor reader is wondering what number word the above example was. (It was the two hundred and nineteenth word, and at the beginning of this very sentence, the two hundred and seventy-third, in case you're curious.)

  A brief note on hyphenation—at this time, it remains unclear (three-hundred and six) whether or not a hyphenated word might count as one or two words. Since the writer is constructing this biography in real-time, it might be difficult to maintain the exact specifications of the meta-textual jokes about the word (not mentioned here, for fear of further damaging my reputation with miscountings and sloppy meta-constructs). I would recommend that if the central theme of this bio fails to achieve the desired effect on the reader, they immediately blame the editorial staff, however, that would be doing the fine gentlemen at this press a grave disservice, as they are forthright, upstanding literary citizens, and do their very best despite inconsiderate authors who enjoy experimenting with formatting to the point where any reasonable person would be very upset indeed.

Michael has written other things, including books with many more words than this. He can be found using the information superhighway. Although the author has a preferred search engine that he uses when looking for information on the internet, it feels presumptuous to tell the reader how to find information on his books, articles, and stories, not to mention his music as Flood Damage and the various performance- and burlesque-related things he does. He lives in Chicago. There is a very handsome cat in his house named Doctor Light and a very lovely girlfriend named Sauda. He loves them both very much. The final sentence approaches. Now it is time to leave the reader with something thematically resonant: "It."

Tiffany Morris is a writer from Nova Scotia. Her horror fiction and poetry has appeared in anthologies from Nosetouch Press, as well as in publications such as *Room Magazine*, *Devolution Z Horror Magazine*, and *Siren's Call eZine*, among others. She also edits for Scrimshaw Obscura. Find her online at http://tiffmorris.com or on Twitter at @tiffmorris.

Michael A. Arnzen (www.gorelets.com) once heard that if you envision your death, then you can't possibly die in that manner. So he keeps writing as many little horrors as fast as he can. If you dig short-shorts, his books *100 Jolts* and *The Gorelets Omnibus* are good places to race the grim reaper alongside him.

Brian Warfield is the author of *Beach Story* and *Ninja Type Person* as well as some stories. His website is http://brianwarfield.weebly.com. This is the longest bio he has ever written. He wrote this bio one year ago. He can see the future and nothing has changed. Well, there are flying cars, but you know that.

John Edward Lawson's novels, short and flash fiction, and poetry have garnered nominations for numerous awards, including the Stoker and Wonderland Awards. In addition to being a founder of Raw Dog Screaming Press and former editor-in-chief of *The Dream People*, he currently serves as vice president of the Diverse Writers and Artists of Speculative Fiction.

Amelia Gulbranson is an author and martial artist from the Pacific Northwest. She got into writing by submitting to anthologies alongside her dad. *Hematopoiesis* is her second work for Carrion Blue 555. She will be in 2nd grade this year.

Jonathan Moon writes terrible dark things for terrible dark times. He has written novels (*HEINOUS, Hollow Mountain Dead*), novellas (*Worms In the Needle, Cannibal Hunter*), collections of short stories and novellas (*Stories To Poke Your Eyes Out To*), and hopes to release poetry in the near future. He eats souls, drinks whiskey, and studies anthropology.

Andy de Fonseca is an author, graphic artist, Fortune 500 company, space enthusiast, wife, mother, nerd, Cheez It lover, Indiana-Jonesian adventurist, tiny dog owner, and imgurian who swims with whales, grapples bears, likes to travel, sword-fights weekly with Inigo Montoya, enjoys movies, makes her own sushi, proposed to the pope, and is a pathological liar.

Editor at Atlantean Publishing for twenty years, **DJ Tyrer** has worked in education and retail, and has been published in magazines such as *Cyaegha* and *Tigershark*, in anthologies *Chilling Horror Stories* (Flame Tree) and *Sorcery & Sanctity: A Homage to Arthur Machen* (Hieroglyphics Press), and has a novella available, *The Yellow House* (Dunhams Manor).
http://djtyrer.blogspot.co.uk/

Betty Rocksteady. Betty Rocksteady.
Betty Rocksteady. Betty Rocksteady.
Betty Rocksteady. Betty Rocksteady.
Betty Rocksteady. Betty Rocksteady.
Betty Rocksteady. Betty Rocksteady.
Betty Rocksteady. Betty Rocksteady.
Betty Rocksteady. Betty Rocksteady.
Betty Rocksteady. Betty Rocksteady.
Betty Rocksteady. Betty Rocksteady.
Betty Rocksteady. Betty Rocksteady.
Betty Rocksteady. Betty Rocksteady.
Betty Rocksteady. Betty Rocksteady.
Betty Rocksteady. Betty Rocksteady.
BETTY FUCKING ROCKSTEADY.

CATALOGUE BLUE 555

CB555-01: 555 Vol. 1: None So Worthy
CB555-02: The Book of Adventures
CB555-03: Mr. Malin and the Night
CB555-04: Haiku Fuck You
CB555-05: 555 Vol. 2: This Head, These Limbs
CB555-06: The Book of Adventures 2
CB555-07: A Terrible Thing

Forthcoming:
CB555-08: 555 Vol. 3: Questions & Cancers
CB555-09: Savage Anesthesia
CB555-10: Plague Gods